Rolls-Royce/The Complete Works

THE WORLDS RECORD FOR A NON-STOP MOTOR RUN BROKEN

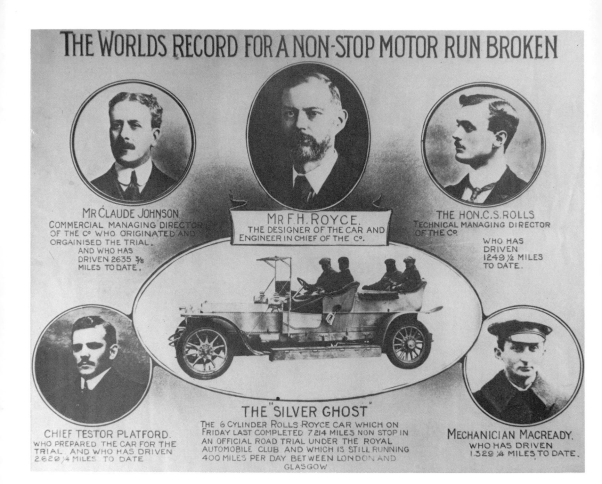

MR CLAUDE JOHNSON.
COMMERCIAL MANAGING DIRECTOR
OF THE Cᵒ WHO ORIGINATED AND
ORGAINISED THE TRIAL,
AND WHO HAS
DRIVEN 2635 ⅜
MILES TO DATE.

MR F.H. ROYCE.
THE DESIGNER OF THE CAR AND
ENGINEER IN CHIEF OF THE Cᵒ.

THE HON.C.S.ROLLS
TECHNICAL MANAGING DIRECTOR
OF THE Cᵒ.

WHO HAS
DRIVEN
1249 ½ MILES
TO DATE.

CHIEF TESTOR PLATFORD.
WHO PREPARED THE CAR FOR THE
TRIAL, AND WHO HAS DRIVEN
2629 ¼ MILES TO DATE

THE "SILVER GHOST"
THE 6 CYLINDER ROLLS-ROYCE CAR WHICH ON
FRIDAY LAST COMPLETED 7214 MILES NON STOP IN
AN OFFICIAL ROAD TRIAL UNDER THE ROYAL
AUTOMOBILE CLUB AND WHICH IS STILL RUNNING
400 MILES PER DAY BETWEEN LONDON AND
GLASGOW

MECHANICIAN MACREADY.
WHO HAS DRIVEN
1.329 ¼ MILES TO DATE.

 *Rolls-Royce*

The Complete Works
The Best 599 Stories about the Worlds Best Car

by MIKE FOX and STEVE SMITH

ff

faber and faber LONDON · BOSTON

First published in 1984
by Faber and Faber Limited
3 Queen Square London WC1N 3AU

Printed in Great Britain by
Fletcher & Son Ltd, Norwich
All rights reserved

© Mike Fox and Steve Smith, 1984

The name ROLLS-ROYCE, the Badge, Radiator Grille
and Mascot are all Registered Trade Marks used
with the kind permission of Rolls-Royce Limited
and Rolls-Royce Motors Limited.

British Library Cataloguing in Publication Data

Fox, Mike
    Rolls-Royce.
    1. Rolls-Royce automobile — Anecdotes,
    facetiae, satire, etc.   2. Automobile
    ownership — Anecdotes, facetiae, satire, etc.
    I. Title   II, Smith, Steve, 19—
    388.3′422   TL215.R6

ISBN 0-571-13363-0
ISBN 0-571-13364-9 Pbk

Library of Congress Cataloging in Publication Data

Fox, Mike.
    Rolls-Royce.

    1. Rolls-Royce automobile.   I. Smith, Steve.
TL215.R6F69 1984   629.2′222   84-13519
ISBN 0-571-13363-0
ISBN 0-571-13364-9 (pbk.)

Dedicated to Lofty Fox
without whom half this book
would never have been written

Dear sir or madam, will you read my book?
John Lennon and Paul McCartney

Contents

Acknowledgements

For permission to reprint copyright·material the authors and publishers gratefully acknowledge:

Chappell & Co. Inc. for a line from 'Who Wants to be a Millionaire' by Cole Porter. Copyright: 1955 & 1956 Buxton Hill Music Corporation, assigned to Chappell & Co. Inc. International Copyright secured. All rights reserved. British Publisher: Chappell Music Limited. Reproduced by permission.

Northern Songs Limited, for a line from 'Paperback Writer' by John Lennon and Paul McCartney.

For permission to reproduce photographs the authors and publishers gratefully acknowledge:

Barnaby's Picture Library: p. 36 (top); BBC Hulton Picture Library: p. 33 (top left); the British Library: pp. 57 (top), 59 and 150; Central Press Photos: p. 147; Fox Photos: p. 115 (lower); Frank Dale and Stepsons of Fulham: p. 44; the *Daily Telegraph* Colour Library: p. 144; Express Newspapers: pp. 46 and 55; Colin Hyams of Hooper & Co. Ltd: p. 135 (bottom); the Keystone Press Agency: pp. 36 (bottom left), 95 and 157; the Raymond Mander and Joe Mitchenson Theatre Collection; p. 33 (top right); the Mansell Collection: p. 151; John Massey Stewart: pp. 23 (2 plates) and 39 (2 plates); the Medina Rajneesh Neo-Sannyas Commune: p. 47 (2 plates); the National Film Archive: p. 45; the National Film Archive and Metro Goldwyn Mayer/United Artists: p. 36 (bottom right); the National Film Archive and Paramount Pictures: p. 43; the National Motor Museum, Beaulieu: p. 26; the Novosti Press Agency: p. 21; the Press Association Limited: pp. 40 and 41; and Eric Barrass and the staff of the Rolls-Royce Museum, Paulerspury.

Preface

The following people and institutions deserve our thanks. All of them helped; none of them bears any responsibility for error:

David Roscoe of Vickers who, with his innumerable stories of Rolls-Royce, provided the original inspiration for this book; David Plastow of Vickers for encouragement over the years; Lewis Gaze of Rolls-Royce Motors for his enormous contribution to the 'Silver Lady' section; Ian Adcock, Roger Cra'ster, Reg Crawford and David Preston for kindly correcting some of the grosser mistakes in the manuscript; Reg Abbis, Bob Cartwright, Dennis Miller-Williams and Peter Ward of Rolls-Royce Motors for incalculable assistance; Guy T. Smith of Rolls-Royce Aero-Engines Limited for information about Rolls-Royce gas turbines; Birmingham's terrific reference library and its helpful staff; Colin Hyams of Hoopers for 24-carat help; Eric Barrass of the Rolls-Royce Enthusiasts Club for photographic help; the Henry Royce Memorial Foundation at Paulerspury; Rolls-Royce Aeronautical Engines of Derby; Miss Mona Mitchell of Buckingham Palace; Art Buchwald for permission to use his article from *More Caviare*; Noel Woodall of Blackpool, the number-plate king, for his omniscience; Matthew Evans of Faber and Faber for his interest and encouragement; Jane Warwick for her part in the original advertisements that led to this book; Neil Anderson of Cogent Elliott, whose disapproval of the whole enterprise acted as a constant spur; Janet Price for the accuracy of her typing, her enormous stamina, and her unbelievable patience; the Archbishop of Canterbury, the Editors of *The Times* and the *Oxford English Dictionary* and Mandy Roget for their diligence in hunting out literals.

We'd also like to thank the scores of authors, editors and biographers whose works we pillaged in our quest for facts. It is not possible to list them all, but it would be inexcusable not to acknowledge the enormous debt we owe to:

Harold Nockold's masterpiece, *The Magic of a Name* (Yeovil, Somerset, G. T. Foulis & Co., 1972).

John M. Fasal's astonishingly erudite compilation, *The Rolls-Royce Twenty* (published privately, 1979). Mr Fasal deserves a mention here as one of the most dedicated Rolls-Royce collectors

13

Bentley Sports Saloon
with coachwork by
Hooper & Co. Ltd., supplied to
H. H. the Maharaja of Mysore

of all time. In 1967 he stopped the Trans-Continental Train in the middle of Australia's Nullarbor Plain, thinking he'd seen a derelict Rolls-Royce. This explanation did little to calm down the ticket inspector – especially as the Rolls-Royce turned out to be a Ford truck. And in 1969 the indefatigable Fasal crossed India in his quest for the automobile equivalent of the Lost Chord: a Rolls-Royce with a centrally placed steering column belonging (legend said) to the Maharaja of Darbangha. Sadly for him, and for our story, it didn't exist.

Richard Garrett's unputdownable *Motoring and the Mighty* (London, Stanley Paul, 1971).

John Webb de Campi's encyclopaedic *Rolls-Royce in America* (London, Dalton Watson, 1975).

Cyris Posthumus's *The Land Speed Record* (London, Osprey, 1971).

Leo Villa and Kevin Desmond's *The World Water Speed Record* (London, Batsford, 1976).

and the indispensable *Autocar* reports.

About this book

This is a book for magpie minds, for chaps who like to buttonhole other chaps in pubs with recondite, if useless, nuggets of information. And since one-third of all pub conversation is about cars, what better subject than the best motor car of all?

In horse-breeding terms the book is out of Ripley's *Believe It or Not* by *The Book of Lists*, with *The Guinness Book of Records* as godfather. If you browse long enough, you'll be able to make your own lists: the most bizarre conversion job? (A bronco-shaped Rolls-Royce body that the Owner rode astride like a horse.) The four funniest men to own one? (Chaplin, Sellers, Wodehouse and Mussolini.) The five best Rolls-Royce fighters? (Dempsey, Ali, Conteh, Rikidozan and Montgomery.) The six richest Owners? (Rockefeller, Morgan, the Nizam of Hyderabad, Tsar Nicholas, the Shah of Persia and our own dear Queen.) The thousand million people least likely to become Owners? (The People's Republic of China.) And so on. As Peter Sellers (an Owner), impersonating Michael Caine (another), said: 'Not a lot of people know that.'

A few marginal notes:

1   Rolls-Royce is insistent in its literature that 'Rolls-Royce' is an adjective, not a noun (not a lot of people know that), and that you shouldn't say 'a Rolls-Royce', but 'a Rolls-Royce motor car', and that you should *never* use the plural 'Rolls-Royces'. If from time to time we have lapsed in this respect, it is in the interests of a more readable literary style. We apologize in advance to the purists.

2   You will find a few – too few, some may say – stories about Bentley in these pages. We are aware of the massive amount of Bentley lore and of the delicate relationship, to put it mildly, between the two marques. Resources of time didn't permit us to give anything like a comprehensive look at W.O.'s marvellous car. Perhaps it might form the subject of another book.

3   The quotations that introduce each of our chapters are all from the writings or sayings or songs of Rolls-Royce Owners.

ROLLS ROYCE

THE BEST SIX-CYLINDER CAR IN THE WORLD?

A FEW REASONS
WHY THE
ROLLS - ROYCE
IS THE
BEST SIX - CYLINDER
CAR IN THE WORLD.

Because of its
(1) Flexibility.
(2) Lightness and cheapness in tyres.
(3) Reliability.
(4) Silence.
(5) Efficiency and cheapness in upkeep.
(6) Safety—brakes, steering gear, etc.
(7) Ease of manipulation, lightness of steering, clutch operation, etc.

A private owner of a R.R. writes:

"I may say my car is a perfect dream. It is so reliable that I have done away with my carriages and horses."

The original of this letter and many other letters from private owners of Rolls Royce cars may be seen at

ROLLS-ROYCE, Ltd.,

14 & 15, CONDUIT STREET, LONDON, W.

Telegrams : "Rolhead, London."

Telephones : 1497 } Gerrard.
1498

AGENTS for LEICESTER, NOTTINGHAM, RUTLAND, AND DERBYSHIRE .. .. The Midland Counties Motor Garage Co., Granby Street, Leices.

AGENTS for NORTH RIDING OF YORKSHIRE AND DURHAM .. .. The Cleveland Car Co., Cleveland Bridge Works, Darlington.

AGENTS, FRANCE .. .. La Société Anonyme "L'Eclaire," 59, Rue la Boëtié, Paris.

AGENTS, UNITED STATES of AMERICA .. .. The Rolls-Royce Import Co., Broadway, New York.

AGENTS, OTTAWA (CANADA) and DISTRICT .. .. Messrs. Ketchum & Co., corner of Bank St. and Sparks St., Ottawa.

 *The Owners*

The only question with wealth is what you do with it.

J. D. Rockefeller

Rolls-Royce Phantom IV with coachwork by H. J. Mulliner & Co. Ltd
built to the special order of H. H. The Shah of Persia

The Owners

You could write a pretty fair history of the twentieth century using only the names of Owners. (Note, by the way, the capital 'O'. An Owner ranks just below the reigning monarch in the Rolls-Royce scheme of things.) True, you'd have to skip Hitler and Gandhi and Schweitzer and most of the popes; but you'd have Lenin and Franco, and Mao and Mussolini; and Chaplin and Garbo and Presley; and Wodehouse and Kipling and Chandler; and Tsar Nicholas II and the Ayatollah Khomeini and most of the crowned heads of Europe; and more famous generals and politicians and mistresses than you could shake a stick at.

To paraphrase Scott Fitzgerald (himself an Owner): 'Rolls-Royce Owners are not like you and me.' They are not. They include some of the richest, cleverest, wickedest, weirdest, wittiest, most charming, most boring, most discriminating, most vulgar human beings ever to climb into a motor car. Their only common denominator: money.

Even there, there are exceptions. You'll read below of the miner on £110 a week basic who became the Owner of a Silver Shadow – and of the king who bought himself a Rolls-Royce and tried to welsh on the deal. But generally speaking, Owners have the green stuff in abundance. They are, as Cole Porter (another Owner) said of his wife, not just rich, but rich rich. And they can afford to make their dreams come true. So in the pages that follow, you'll find the princess who decided that what she wanted parked in her drive was a Rolls-Royce plated – down to the exhaust pipe – in 24-carat gold; the Frenchman who conceived the gruesome idea of having the body of his car in wood – clinker built, and shaped like the rear end of a boat; the maharaja who thought it would be neat to have his steering wheel made of elephant tusks; and the Eastern holy man, devoted to a life of contemplation, who decided that what he'd like to contemplate was forty-seven Silver Spurs, in which he found the peace that passeth understanding.

Welcome, then, to a sort of Rolls-Royce menagerie: a collection of the most outrageous, the most famous and the most eccentric Owners in eighty years of Rolls-Royce history. . . .

*   *   *

Right from the very beginning, Charlie Rolls was wowing the titled and the famous with Royce's silent new creation. In 1905 he rounded up a bunch of Old Etonian chums and persuaded them that what they should give Dr Warre (Eton's redoubtable headmaster) on his retirement was one of the new-fangled 3-cylinder 15 h.p. Rolls-Royces. Within twelve months of meeting Royce, his list of clients read like a combination of *Debrett* and the *Almanach de Gotha*: the Crown Prince of Romania, Princess Blucher, Prince D'Arenberg, Prince Potenzia, the Duke of Sutherland, the Duke of Manchester, Lord Raglan, the Earl of Verulam, Lord Dunsany, Sir Thomas Lipton, et cetera, et cetera.

*   *   *

The very first Owner after the formation of the Rolls-Royce company in 1906 was a minor celebrity: Paris E. Singer. Paris (he got his bizarre name because his globe-trotting old man called his offspring by the name of the town where they happened to be born – hence his brother Washington, also an Owner) took delivery of a dark-green Rolls-Royce – with a rear entrance. Mr Singer was the heir to the Singer sewing-machine millions, quite a few of which he lavished on Isadora Duncan, the dancer. Second in the Rolls-Royce Hall of Fame was Sir Oswald Mosley, Bt.; and third, a Guinness.

*   *   *

Among the first Royals to become Owners were the Russians. In 1913 Tsar Nicholas II bought two Silver Ghosts (his third was completed in 1918, by which time he was a prisoner of the Bolsheviks); his mother, the Dowager Empress Marie, owned a 1914 laundaulet (maroon, with the imperial monogram on each door); and more interestingly, Prince Felix Yusopov had a Rolls-Royce side-light cabriolet in which he and his fellow conspirators transported the body of Rasputin to a hole in the ice of the River Neva – after dosing him with enough cyanide for twelve, shooting him several times, then clubbing him almost to death. ('Almost' because, astonishingly, the Russian police said that what the mad monk eventually died from was drowning.)

If you're wondering about the Tsar's third Rolls-Royce, the one completed after he became a prisoner, it was taken over by the British War Office and used for transporting VIPs around London.

*   *   *

Lewis J. Zeleznick fled the Tsar's pogroms, made it to Hollywood, changed his name to Selznick *en route*, and became one of the first movie moguls. He also became a quadruple Owner. In 1918

Rasputin

he cabled the Tsar, as one Rolls-Royce Owner to another: WHEN I WAS A BOY IN RUSSIA YOUR POLICE TREATED MY PEOPLE VERY BAD HOWEVER NO HARD FEELINGS. HEAR YOU ARE NOW OUT OF WORK. IF YOU WILL COME TO NEW YORK CAN GIVE YOU FINE ACTING POSITION IN PICTURES. SALARY NO OBJECT. REPLY MY EXPENSE. REGARDS YOU AND FAMILY. SELZNICK.

The 'position' Selznick had in mind was a starring role in his next film, *The Fall of the Romanovs*.

*   *   *

A year after Rasputin's death, as he'd predicted, came the end of the Romanovs – but not the end of Rolls-Royce motor cars in Russia. In a Moscow museum today you can see chassis number 16X. It's a 1919 Silver Ghost; it was exhibited at the 1920 London Motor Show, and its owner was Vladimir Ilich Lenin. In fact, Lenin (through Leonid Krassin, his man in London) ordered *nine* Rolls-Royces. Three of them still exist today – one of them being the only Rolls-Royce in the world fitted with half-tracks, which permitted the father of the Russian Revolution to get about in the snow, in style. Vladimir Ilich loved journeying by car as a means of relaxation. By night he slept in barns; by day he travelled like a millionaire.

*   *   *

21

Stalin owned a Rolls-Royce too; and so did Leonid Brezhnev. In 1979 Brezhnev, a well-known automobile collector, had a black Rolls-Royce sent to Vienna for his personal use during the meetings with President Carter.

*   *   *

Over the years there has been a steady (if microscopically small) trickle of Rolls-Royces through the Iron Curtain. In 1971 the Russians ordered two Silver Shadows and two Bentleys, and in 1983 a Silver Spirit followed.

*   *   *

At the other end of the political spectrum, but almost as unexpected an Owner as Lenin, was Henry Ford. He bought a Silver Ghost in 1924. When the bowler-hatted Rolls-Royce service engineers appeared at his door a year later for their usual 12-monthly check, he was so amazed he cabled Royce, 'After I've sold one of *my* cars I don't want to see it or hear of it again!' It is also said that when Ford went to visit a friend in his Silver Ghost, he explained, 'My Ford was being serviced, so I came in the next best thing!'

*   *   *

Pre-dating the Russians and the Americans were the most uninhibited Owners of all: the maharajas of India.

In 1908 the Maharaja of Gwalior saw the dazzlingly beautiful 'Pearl of India' Rolls-Royce exhibited at the Bombay Motor Show. He fell in love, bought it for rubies from a shrewd Lancastrian called Frank Norbury, and started a mania that lasted forty years among rich Indians for acquiring Rolls-Royces. And no wonder, for the 'Pearl of India' was perhaps the most beautiful Rolls-Royce ever built. It was finished in cream with apple-green stripes edged with gold. The brown leather upholstery was matched by a set of brown leather Finnegan trunks, carried on the roof rack. The spare tyre had its own matching brown leather case. Outside the rear of the car was a seat for the Maharaja's manservant. And to demonstrate that such beauty was founded on brilliant engineering, the 'Pearl' was entered into one of the toughest driving tests possible: the Bombay to Kohlapur rally – 120 dusty bumpy miles through six mountain passes in the Western Ghats with no stops, no spares and a locked bonnet. The 'Pearl' strolled it with miles to spare, making it the most luxurious car ever to win an endurance race, and the Rolls-Royce mania grew.

*   *   *

Lenin's Rolls-Royce in the grounds of the Kremlin . . .

. . . and converted for use in the snow with half tracks and skis

23

Subsequent Indian Owners were considerably less restrained in their tastes than the Maharaja of Gwalior. No excess of ornamentation was too lavish, no refinement too costly for these staggeringly wealthy men.

The Maharaja of Nandagoons's Rolls-Royce had a steering wheel made from elephants' tusks; all the other controls were carved from ivory; and in the rear was an ornate throne covered with damask silk.

*   *   *

The Maharaja of Bharatpur had his Rolls-Royce fitted with searchlights for tiger shooting, and extra-wide running boards to carry his tiger hunters. The interior fittings were in solid gold, silver and mother-of-pearl; the panelling was in mahogany with a satin veneer inlaid with mother-of-pearl, and the upholstery covered in mauve silk shot with silver.

*   *   *

The Nizam of Hyderabad had a yellow Rolls-Royce with golden lace curtains, gold brocade upholstery, a solid silver cupola in the roof, and of course, a throne. He also had an interior built with a roof looking like the heavens at night (a small miracle achieved by the coachbuilders using fairy lights and a perforated blue false ceiling). In its long life, it has covered just 345 miles.

*   *   *

One of the Maharaja of Patiala's Rolls-Royces had an instrument board encrusted with precious jewels. When it went in for a service, four men stood over it on 24-hour armed guard; and when he drove in it the Maharaja, as if to compete with his car, wore a pearl necklace insured by Lloyds for a million pounds, and a breastplate set with a thousand and one diamonds. He also wore underpants costing £200 a pair. His annual underpants budget, it is reported, was £31,000.

*   *   *

Surpassing them all, in everything (except perhaps good taste), was the Maharaja of Vizianagaram. His most cherished Rolls-Royce was said to be made of silver. Each year it was the high point of the Vizianagaram state procession: a hundred cars, a thousand elephants – and a silver Rolls-Royce, which he blessed in a shower of rose petals. (Although if you think blessing a Rolls-Royce is the sort of freaky thing only foreigners get up to, then you ought to know that in 1978 the Reverend John Richardson, Vicar of St Mary's Church in Nantwich, Cheshire, blessed a Silver Shadow as part of the harvest festival. A member of the congregation remarked that it was going in for its first service.)

*   *   *

The Maharana of Udaipur had his Rolls-Royce Twenty adapted to a jeep body. And all the instruments on the Maharana's 1923 Barker tourer were hand operated; he was paralysed from the waist down.

*   *   *

One Indian prince had his Rolls-Royce crowned with a thatched roof.

*   *   *

The Raja of Bwalpur commanded that when he rode in his state car all passers-by should turn their backs on him.

*   *   *

Shumoon Abdulali of Bombay, one of the best-known orchid growers in India, wasn't a maharaja, but his eccentricity deserves a mention. He kept a 6½-foot rat snake in his 1927 Barker tourer – to inhibit mice. On one journey the unfortunate reptile travelled a considerable distance coiled around the revolving prop shaft. On another, Mr Abdulali travelled from Mahabaleshwar to Bombay with thirty-six hens and a live deer in the back – 200 difficult (and noisy) miles.

*   *   *

The ruler of Alwar owned six Silver Ghosts. Rolls-Royce refused to carry out certain modifications, so the old man, in an unbelievable fit of pique, had all six converted into garbage trucks.

*   *   *

In 1935, a Phantom II was delivered to Nepal. It was carried across vertiginous gorges and mountain passes by 200 porters; it crossed raging torrents on giant rafts. It became the first Rolls-Royce in Kathmandu. But it was by no means the last. The Queen Mothers (note the plural!) of Nepal subsequently had a Bentley Mk V delivered.

*   *   *

Mr R. N. Matthewson of Calcutta was *not* a Rolls-Royce Owner, but his car is worthy of note. It was adapted to look like a giant swan, with snapping beak and appropriate sound effects. Not content with this imaginative exterior, he had a fully operative pedal organ installed in the interior.

*   *   *

Some Indian potentates' titles were as ornate as their cars. Patiala's full name was 'Lieutenant-General His Highness Farzand-i-Khas-i-Daulat-i-Inglishia, Mansur-i-Zaman, Amir-ul-Umra, Maharaja Dhiraj Raj Rajeshwar Shree, Maharaja-i-

More people have travelled
in this model than any other

Rajgan, Maharaja Sir Bhupindra Singh, Mohinder Bahadur, Yadu Vanshavatans Bhatti Kul Bhushan, Maharaja Dhiraj of Patiala, GCSI, GCIE, GCVO, GBE.' He probably used a shorter version on his cheques.

*   *   *

King Amanullah of Afghanistan, who you'd think would have had a few afghanis (at 45 afghanis to the dollar) to rub together, was a disappointment. In 1928 King Amanullah and his entourage made an official visit to Rolls-Royce. After an inordinate amount of ceremony and a lot of encouragement from the chaps at the Foreign Office, he took personal delivery of a royal-blue open tourer, bodywork by Barkers of Mayfair. They had a terrible time getting him to send the cheque.

*   *   *

The Maharaja of Mysore had thirty-five Rolls-Royces (and created a new collective noun: a 'Mysore' of Rolls-Royces). The Maharaja of Patiala had thirty-eight, and a single enormous garage containing twenty-three of them. He also had a resident Rolls-Royce engineer, Mr Harold Whyman, who later became Rolls-Royce's man in Shrewsbury.

*   *   *

Amassing Rolls-Royce motor cars is clearly an expensive business – but the record isn't held by a maharaja or a nizam or a nawab or even Bhagwan Shree Rajneesh of Rajneeshpuram,

The Louis XIV Rolls-Royce

And inside

USA (whose followers, as you'll read below, recently presented him with his forty-seventh), the People's Republic of China (who in 1951 placed an order for six), or Stanley Sears whose collection of some of the most exquisite examples of the marque ever made was auctioned by Christie's in 1983. The Rolls-Royce collecting record – you could guess for a year without getting close – is held by the Scottish Co-operative Society. In the 1960s they had a fleet of 240, which they used almost exclusively for funerals and weddings. One of their largest single orders, for thirty Rolls-Royces, specified 'without heaters or radios', which mystified the Rolls-Royce sales department. The Co-op's explanation: 'Most of our customers take only one ride in them.'

*   *   *

Nor did the maharajas have a monopoly on ornamentation. In 1927, a Mr Gasque, senior executive of Woolworth's, bought a Rolls-Royce Phantom I, some authentic Louis XIV furniture, and asked Clarke of Wolverhampton to combine the two. The result was one of the most elegant Rolls-Royces of all time. The rear seat is a Louis-XIV sofa covered with Aubusson *petit point*; the ceiling (by a French artist) is decorated with cupids and roses; the accessories, from coach lamps to ashtrays, are in solid silver; the division between passenger and driver is a Louis-XIV cabinet surmounted by an ormolu clock; the cabinet contains a crystal liqueur set and a cigar box; the exterior bodywork is finished in a pleasing basketwork design. And the whole thing was just to please a lady – in this case, Mr Gasque's wife, who received it as a birthday gift.

*   *   *

Giving away Rolls-Royces is not all that rare. In 1980, a grateful Iranian lady went into Jack Barclay's with a Safeway's bag full of £20 notes. With them she purchased a brand new Silver Shadow which she then left outside a London hospital. On the driving wheel, a short note addressed to her surgeon. It said, simply, 'Thank you.'

*   *   *

After the liberation of The Netherlands, Queen Wilhelmina rewarded General Patton with a gift of her 1926 black and primrose Phantom I. He never drove it. He had it crated and shipped to a warehouse, where it was discovered after his death.

*   *   *

The only case on record of anyone *finding* a Rolls-Royce was that of Lieutenant-Commander Leycester RN, who in 1918 found a gleaming Rolls-Royce, chassis no. 2503, abandoned on the quayside at the Russian port of Odessa – presumably left behind by some White Russian émigré in a hurry.

*   *   *

The most careless Owner on record must be the unnamed Cheshire businessman who reported to the company in 1909 that he had lost his Rolls-Royce 'somewhere in Belgium'.

*   *   *

Mr Mathey, of Johnson Mathey the bullion merchants, bought a Silver Ghost in 1925. He had all oil and water pipes, the oil tank and other parts that were normally copper-plated, plated in platinum.

*   *   *

A Scottish Owner had the key for his Rolls-Royce made in solid gold.

*   *   *

Hooper's are at the moment preparing a Silver Spirit for a Middle Eastern princess that has all the brightwork (i.e., everything that would normally be chromium-plated or stainless steel) plated in 24-carat gold, down to the exhaust pipe! The windows are gold tinted. Inside the car all the woodwork, including the fascia, is covered with gold leaf. The seats have gold-leaf piping and are embossed with the coat of arms of the royal family – in gold leaf.

*   *   *

The eccentric, pugnacious and colourful (literally) Yellow Earl, Lord Lonsdale, had a succession of cars, all yellow. He was president of the Automobile Association (hence its house colours); of Bertram Mills's Circus, and of Arsenal Football Club, and he claimed to have once knocked out the redoubtable John L. Sullivan. His favourite car was a yellow 1923 Rolls-Royce 20 h.p. On finding he couldn't get into the car without taking off his top hat, His Lordship had a (taller) 1910 Daimler body grafted on to his car. This car – in which Lord Lonsdale visited every racecourse in Britain – was auctioned at Christie's in 1983. Incidentally, this particular Lonsdale is the chap who gave his name to boxing's Lonsdale Belt.

*   *   *

A different solution to the hat problem was devised by a British diplomat's wife in Pakistan. She, unable to wear her hat in the car, had a hole cut under her seat so it could be lowered. Depressingly for her husband, the car became known in diplomatic circles as the Flying Thunderbox.

*   *   *

William Randolph Hearst, the newspaper king (and model for Orson Welles's 'Citizen Kane'), had two Rolls-Royce cars, the insides of which were miniature saloons. Each one had a mirrored-glass interior, a bar, a table – and a roll-top desk.

* * *

In 1948 Mrs Churchill Wylie had her Phantom fitted with a bar, a writing desk, a gramophone, a picnic set, a cigar cabinet and (in the boot) a wash-basin with matching mirror, towel hanger and soap holder.

* * *

Jack Barclay (racing driver and founder of the largest Rolls-Royce salesroom in Britain) had a backgammon board in rare wood fitted into his Rolls-Royce.

* * *

An unnamed Owner recently had not one, but two television sets installed in the rear compartment of his Corniche – one facing forward, the other backwards. Another had expensive alterations made to his car because he wanted an extra-heavy stone ashtray fitted on which he could knock out his pipe.

* * *

Another anon had a collapsible bath and a commode fitted.

* * *

Mr Ken Durran of Market Harborough, Leicestershire, has a sable and brown Silver Shadow on the sides and boot of which are painted, in sepia, portraits of four vintage Rolls-Royce motor cars.

* * *

In the less peaceful parts of the world, anti-terrorist Rolls-Royces are the vogue. In February 1984, BBC Television featured an Asian Owner whose Phantom can be electrified at the press of a button. Anyone then touching the exterior receives a very nasty shock.

* * *

Possibly the least pleasing piece of Rolls-Royce decoration happened to chassis no. 45J, which for a time was owned by King Farouk of Egypt. Built in 1914 for an unknown Frenchman, it was handed over to the German coachbuilders Schapiro-Sebera, who had the very bad idea of giving it a clinker-built boat body. The effect is unpleasing in the extreme. Rivalling it, though, is the gruesome Silver Wraith commissioned from Hooper's by Nubar Gulbenkian. The whole car, including the

It might be more aerodynamic than an Audi 100 but it's also the ugliest Rolls-Royce ever. It was built on a Silver Wraith chassis by Hooper's, for Nubar Gulbenkian

wheels and the famous radiator, was entombed in a bronze two-tone 'modern' streamlined body with a curved radiator grille. Hidden door handles gave the whole horrid edifice a perfectly smooth appearance, like something out of *Flash Gordon*. As *Autocar* commented in 1947 (with some restraint), 'Not everyone will care for the very advanced appearance – but there is no doubt it is very striking.'

The ineffably wealthy Gulbenkian, you'll recall, was also famous for his exotic adaptations of London taxis, about one of which he said: 'It'll turn on a sixpence – whatever that is.' But when he asked if the famous radiator might grace one of these taxi adaptations, the men from Rolls-Royce, no doubt repressing a shudder, firmly declined.

In 1955 things changed for the free-spending Nubar. His more frugal father, Calouste ('Mr Five per cent') Gulbenkian, died, having changed his will so that Nubar was cut off with only a million.

*   *   *

An Australian Owner had his 1926 Twenty fitted with an enormous (and revolting) wooden caravan body. John Fasals in his excellent book, *The Rolls-Royce Twenty*, calls it the original Sweet Lavinia, the Gutless Wonder.

*   *   *

31

The *lèse-majesté* is endless. In 1927 Mr Arthur Nape, a Mansfield, Nottinghamshire, pork butcher, was mentioned in the press for carrying pigs in the back of his Rolls-Royce. When an emissary from the company discreetly inquired if this practice was absolutely necessary, Mr Nape gave him the majestic reply, 'Pigs bought it; pigs'll ride in it.'

*   *   *

As you might imagine, Rolls-Royce is pretty good at preserving the anonymity of its customers, so some of the best stories about Owners must be attributed to Anon. It was an anonymous Italian Owner who in 1948, wishing to make some modifications to his car, commissioned a seance to call up the spirit of Henry Royce. Rolls-Royce legend has it that the advice from beyond the veil was: 'Consult your authorized distributor.'

*   *   *

And it was an Australian Anon who had a sliding partition installed in the interior of his Rolls-Royce to prevent the sheep he often carried in the back from licking his ear.

*   *   *

The most dedicated Owner of all, however, was by no means anonymous. Miss Letitia Overend of Dundrum, near Dublin, probably held the world record for driving the same car continually. Miss Overend drove her blue 20 h.p. Rolls-Royce tourer every day for fifty-one years. It is said that when in the 1950s she complained of back trouble, her doctor's advice was that instead of cranking her car by hand she should invest in an electric self-starter. Letitia died in 1978; the car is still being driven by her sister Naomi.

*   *   *

In 1956 Baron Raben-Levetzau of Aalholm Castle, Denmark, heard rumours that behind a wall on his estate was a mysterious, ancient motor car of impeccable pedigree. Sceptical but intrigued he ordered the wall to be taken down. To his astonished gaze was revealed a beautiful 1911 Silver Ghost. It had been walled up thirty years earlier by a disgruntled Owner, who was unwilling to accept what he regarded as a derisory offer for the vehicle.

*   *   *

Among the cars attending the memorial service for the sculptor Rodin at Westminster Abbey in 1917, none attracted more attention than that belonging to the patriotic Lady Westminster. In order to save petrol at a time of war, she had the top of her 40/50 limousine fitted with a sort of barrage balloon attachment in order that it could run on gas.

*   *   *

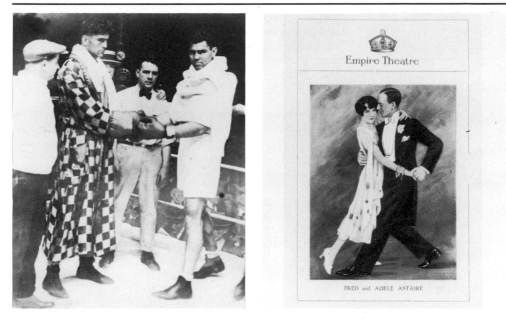

(*left*) Jack Dempsey – on the right of the photograph – v. Louis Firpo, 1923. To celebrate his victory Dempsey bought his first Rolls-Royce

(*right*) Programme cover for *Lady, Be Good,* the show that made enough money for Fred Astaire to buy his first Rolls-Royce

Otto Oppenheimer, the diamond merchant, had a Rolls-Royce Phantom I called *The Black Diamond.* It was built with secret compartments, the location of which was known only to himself and the engineers at Derby. The car was used for carrying hundreds of thousands of pounds' worth of uncut diamonds from source to market.

*   *   *

On 14 September 1923 at the Polo Grounds, New York, in what is generally acknowledged to have been the most sensational heavyweight fight of all time, Jack Dempsey, the Manassa Mauler, was knocked clean out of the ring and into the press seats in the first round of his title fight with 'Wild Bull of the Pampas', Luis Angel Firpo. Snarling, Dempsey clambered back and annihilated Firpo in round 2. To celebrate his epic victory, the Mauler ordered a Rolls-Royce.

Dempsey became hopelessly addicted to Rolls-Royces; he bought six in all, equalling the number of successful fights he had for the world title.

*   *   *

The next world heavyweight champion to own a Rolls-Royce was Muhammad Ali. A member of his entourage said, 'It floats like a butterfly.'

*   *   *

33

Apart from Emperor Hirohito, in Japan one of the biggest Rolls-Royce fans was Rikidozan. Riki (as very few people dared call him) weighed in at 24 stone (336 pounds), and was to Sumo wrestling what Ali was to boxing. Sadly, he was killed in a knife fight in 1964 – but not before he had bought two Rolls-Royces.

*   *   *

The most married millionaire of all time was Tommy Manville Jr. He was almost as fond of Rolls-Royce cars as he was of wives; having ten of the former and eleven of the latter. It is probable that he kept his Rolls-Royces longer than he kept his brides. (His seventh wife, for example, lasted $7\frac{1}{2}$ hours.)

*   *   *

Gordon Selfridge, the London department-store genius ('The customer is always right'), made a fortune in business – and lost all of it on showgirls and gambling. His favourite expression: 'I'll bet you a Rolls-Royce you're wrong!' He often lost his bets.

*   *   *

In 1926 Fred and Adele Astaire came from New York to the Empire Theatre, London, in their dazzling dancing hit *Lady Be Good* (and the aforementioned Gordon Selfridge paid £50 to dance with Adele). They became the toast of London and, by the time they went back on SS *Homeric*, they had earned enough to take a Rolls-Royce with them.

Adele married into the aristocracy. Fred just did as best he could as a song-and-dance man. At least he made enough money to buy three more Rolls-Royces.

*   *   *

In 1927 Warner Brothers asked Broadway star Al Jolson (their second choice) to appear in an experimental movie – with sound. The film was *The Jazz Singer*, the world's first talking picture. Jolson's immortal words: 'You ain't heard nothin' yet!' thrilled millions, and 'Jolie' made $75,000, plus a gift of a Rolls-Royce from the delighted Warner Brothers. Next year Jolson had little Davey Lee climb up on his knee while he sang 'Sonny Boy' in *The Singing Fool*. The Warner Brothers made a fortune from the two films – and all of them bought Rolls-Royces.

The 'Singing Fool' became nearly as addicted to Rolls-Royces as Dempsey. He had four in six years.

*   *   *

One of the first Owners in Hollywood was Mary Pickford. Her 1926 Phantom I had a secret liquor store to baffle Prohibition agents.

*   *   *

Marlene Dietrich with her car
during the filming of *Morocco*

Jackie Coogan, child star of silent films, established a record by
owning two Rolls-Royces before he was 21. His father, sharing
his son's precocious success, became the first Rolls-Royce dealer
in Southern California.

*   *   *

Not until the seventies did anyone challenge Coogan's record.
Then along came the Maharaja Ji, guru of the Divine Light Mis-
sion. He was a pudgy 14-year-old when his English followers
('We like to give him the best') bought him a gold-painted Rolls-
Royce. One of his disciples explained the seeming incongruity
thus: 'It's like Christ riding into Jerusalem on a donkey.' (For
an echo of this, see below, the Reverend Ike.)

*   *   *

In the early part of her career Diana Dors was a precocious Rolls-
Royce Owner. She was 20 and almost broke, but with a magnificent gesture of confidence in the future she went out and ordered
a black Rolls-Royce on the never-never, thus becoming the
youngest Owner in the United Kingdom.

*   *   *

In 1912, Fred Karno, director of the troupe of funny men that spawned Chaplin and Stan Laurel, took delivery of a cobalt-violet Rolls-Royce that was remarkable at the time – for having windows that could be raised and lowered 'by turning a small handle on the inside'.

*   *   *

Constance Bennett, the movie queen, owned a Rolls-Royce (with a velvet interior) and a well-developed ego. For the delectation of her fans, Miss Bennett had a special adaptation fitted: an interior spotlight, permanently focused on herself.

*   *   *

Ecdysiast Gypsy Rose Lee, the pioneer of striptease, was involved in a crash in her Rolls-Royce while travelling in rural Yugoslavia. Since the crash was clearly her fault, she was astonished to see the other driver and his passenger fleeing in obvious terror. On reaching her destination she quizzed her hosts about this melodramatic scene. 'Simple,' they replied. 'There are at the moment only three Rolls-Royces in Yugoslavia. The other two belong to President Tito.'

*   *   *

On 2 February 1944 Augustus John began a portrait of General Montgomery, then Commander-in-Chief of British Forces in Europe. Monty was deeply suspicious of the painter: 'He drinks, he's dirty, and I know there are woman in the background.' He was persuaded to continue only when George Bernard Shaw, the playwright, was brought to Chelsea by Monty's Rolls-Royce, to reassure him.

*   *   *

Guess what Mussolini, George Bernard Shaw and Zsa Zsa Gabor have in common?

One of the great society scandals of the war years happened in 1944, when actor-manager Ivor Novello, darling of the theatre, was imprisoned in Wormwood Scrubs for one month for unpatriotically driving his Rolls-Royce without a wartime petrol permit.

*   *   *

George ('When I'm cleaning windows') Formby was for a goodish number of years the most highly paid entertainer in Britain. His wife, Beryl, kept him on an astonishingly tight rein, allowing him, it is said, only five shillings a week pocket money. She did, however, permit him one pleasing extravagance. Each year the car-crazy comedian was allowed to buy two cars. Inevitably one of them was always a Rolls-Royce.

*   *   *

Zsa Zsa ('I never hated a man enough to give him back his diamonds') Gabor had a Rolls-Royce that originally belonged to the Duchess of Kent. It was 'styled' for Zsa Zsa by George Barris of Kustom Industries. The mascot is gold-plated; the car is finished in thirty coats of Murano Pearl of Essene two-tone gold paint. The Rolls-Royce radiator badge bears Zsa Zsa's signature. It contains a walnut wine cabinet with 24-carat gold goblets bearing Zsa Zsa's signature in jewels and a gold-inlaid walnut make-up cabinet with gold-plated hair brushes. It was bought at a Hollywood car auction in 1983 by Mr Henry Kurtz of the Krazy Kar Museum, New Jersey. (He also bought the original Batmobile 'for my son to drive'.)

*   *   *

Michael Caine bought a Rolls-Royce before he could drive. One happy day, when he was first making it big in the movies, his accountant telephoned him with the glad tidings that he was now a millionaire. Caine, who was just setting out to do the weekend shopping, added to his back-of-an-envelope list: razor blades, cornflakes, pound of butter, loaf of bread, Rolls-Royce. In jeans and plimsolls, and unshaven, he and an actor mate were turned down at the first showroom they visited, as not seeming like serious candidates for the world's finest car. In his biography *Raising Caine* Caine tells of how he bought a beautiful convertible at their next stop, and of how he took great pleasure in being driven slowly past the original showroom, with the top down, giving joyful V-signs to the incredulous salesman.

*   *   *

The only case of a Rolls-Royce attempting to replace its owner was recorded in this advertisement in *The Times*: 'TITLED MOTOR CAR WISHES TO DISPOSE OF OWNER. 1958 Rolls-Royce Silver

Cloud seeks new owner of distinction after small, meticulous, but non-U mileage. Rather tired of being conducted by professional funny man and his chauffeur, neither of whom appears in *Debrett*. Deliverance: £5,250.' The professional funny man was Peter Sellers, who replaced the discontented Silver Cloud by a Bentley Continental with two-way telephone.

*   *   *

Elaine Stritch (of a Rolls-Royce that transported her from hotel to theatre): 'So I got into this living room and came over here.'

*   *   *

Barry Sheene, supreme motorcyclist: 'It's the only half-decent thing Britain still makes.'

*   *   *

Keith Moon, drummer of the Who, was a good customer of Rolls-Royce but an erratic driver, as was demonstrated the day he sold his lavishly appointed house. The morning after he moved out, Moon received a frantic phone call from the new owner. 'There's a Rolls-Royce in the swimming pool!' he complained. 'Oh yeh, forgot to tell you. I took a right when I should've took a left. Sorry,' replied the imperturbable Loon.

*   *   *

Cary Grant hates to be caught without a Rolls-Royce. He had (and maybe still has) three Rolls-Royces garaged separately in Hollywood, New York and London (the last number-plated CG1).

*   *   *

John Lennon's Rolls-Royce had a bed in the back, and Aristotle Onassis's had a refrigerator.

*   *   *

The Beatles' psychedelic Rolls-Royce elicited two notable comments, one from the heraldic artist who turned down the job of decorating it: 'It's not heraldry – it's sacrilege!', and one from Rolls-Royce: 'It is not the company's policy to comment on Owners' tastes.'

*   *   *

Jimmy Savile, the radio and TV personality with a heart of gold, surprised his Rolls-Royce distributor by walking 50 miles from London to Eastbourne (for charity, of course) to pick up his first Corniche. For what happened when he arrived, see 'The Silver Lady'.

*   *   *

Elvis had two Rolls-Royce cars – but he bought his mother a 1957 pink Cadillac.

*   *   *

Lenin was always pleased to share his Rolls-Royce with exuberant village children.
(Painting from a contemporary Soviet magazine)

Lenin's Rolls-Royce
in the Lenin Museum,
Moscow

Sammy Davis Jr bought his first hundred-thousand-dollar Rolls-Royce sight unseen, from an artist's impression of the vehicle.

*　　*　　*

In September 1981, impressionist Mike Yarwood's red Silver Shadow was stolen from the Royal Garden Hotel, Kensington, London, while he was recording a TV show. A few days later, adorned with false number plates (LSD 777), it was used in a dramatic armed robbery at Kutchinsky, a jeweller's in Bond Street. The miscreants, wearing monkey masks, got away with half a million pounds in jewellery – but not Mr Yarwood's Rolls-Royce. That they contrived to bounce off a half-dozen other cars parked in Mayfair. One, a Jaguar, was towed 50 yards before both cars were abandoned. The Rolls-Royce's paintwork was scratched and the radiator sadly buckled. Mike commented gloomily: 'I can't bear to look at it.'

*　　*　　*

In *Dallas* Howard Keel, as Clayton Farlow, became the first Texan to own a Silver Spirit. It is *not* true that when he saw the fabled Connolly leather seats he carolled, 'Bless your beautiful hide'.

In *Dynasty*, Krystle Carrington (Linda Evans) drives a Corniche.

*　　*　　*

Peter Sellers owned over 100 cars – including a string of Rolls-Royces. In 1968, in Belgravia, London, he accomplished the rare feat of crashing his silver Rolls-Royce (bought from Terence Rattigan) into another Rolls-Royce, reportedly in a fit of anger about something his passenger, Miranda Quarry, had said.

*　　*　　*

One of our favourite boxers, former light-heavyweight champion John Conteh, managed a spectacular shunt in

Piccadilly, London, just outside Fortnum and Mason, in the small hours of 22 November 1978. Emerging from a well-known club, John and his Rolls-Royce delivered some fearsome body blows to six parked cars, leaving them in the same state as the Scouse scrapper used to leave most of his opponents.

*   *   *

The world's record for crashing a Rolls-Royce is held by Larry Flynt, publisher of *Hustler* magazine. After taking delivery of his new Rolls-Royce, he managed three collisions in the first twenty minutes. (For more spectacular crashes, see 'Apocrypha'.)

*   *   *

Tony Thompson, Rolls-Royce's man in Beverly Hills, California, sold sixty-five Rolls-Royces in 1983. Astonishingly, sixty-one of his customers paid cash.

*   *   *

A Mr Wheat of Texas is probably the only Owner with his own petrol station in the drive. His drive is $172\frac{1}{2}$ miles long.

*   *   *

One of John Mills's earliest films was *Car of Dreams* (1935) with Robertson Hare. In it he plays the lucky hundred-thousandth customer of the firm who wins a beautiful Sedanca de Ville Rolls-Royce. The film ends on a note of fantasy with a trip through the clouds in the Rolls-Royce.

*   *   *

In *Those Magnificent Men in their Flying Machines* Robert Morley is featured as the driver of an old Rolls-Royce. It was in fact the most famous car of all – the original, beautiful, Silver Ghost.

*   *   *

In *The Abominable Dr Phibes* Vincent Price kills David Hutcheson by freezing him to death with an ice-making machine installed in the back of his Rolls-Royce.

*   *   *

Easily the most shocking end to a Rolls-Royce occurs in *The Long Good Friday*, starring Bob Hoskins. As part of a gang war, Bob's mum's Rolls-Royce is blown to bits outside her church, and her chauffeur Eric is distributed over a large part of East London.

*   *   *

In *The Great Gatsby* Robert Redford drives a Phantom I Ascot tourer.

*   *   *

'The rich are different from us.' Robert Redford as F. Scott Fitzgerald's hero, Gatsby

The yellow Rolls-Royce
(as seen in the film
of the same name)

In *The Yellow Rolls-Royce* the original car used in filming was a yellow Barker-bodied Phantom II. But sharp-eyed Rolls-Royce watchers will observe that the car changes at least twice in the course of filming. (Clue: the position of the spare wheel.)

*　　*　　*

In *The Four Horsemen of the Apocalypse* Glenn Ford owns a Phantom II (74 MY) which also appeared in *The Man from U.N.C.L.E.*

*　　*　　*

In The Red Shoes Anton Walbrook also owns a Phantom II (24 PY).

*　　*　　*

In 1926 the screen's greatest lover, Rudolph Valentino, died. While millions sobbed, he went to his grave in New York with a cortège of eighteen Rolls-Royces.

*　　*　　*

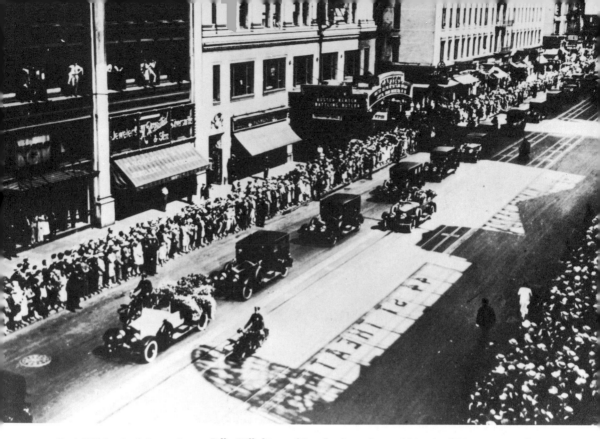

Rudolf Valentino's funeral
cortège: eighteen
Rolls-Royce cars

Billy Hill, king of London's underworld in the fifties, arranged a gangster's funeral for his lieutenant, knife artist Billy Blythe, in 1957. It involved 3,000 mourners, 250 wreaths, a silver embossed coffin – and a cortège of twelve Rolls-Royces.

* * *

Otto Zackey, a miner of New Moston, Manchester, England, turned up for his shift in April 1981 driving a two-tone Silver Shadow. He'd traded in his previous car and his savings from thirty-five years of colliery work to realize a dream. 'I thought I'd buy the best,' he said.

* * *

In March 1984, the *Sun* newspaper reported, under the headline 'NO BIRDS, NO BOOZE, NO FAGS – BUT WHAT A MOTOR!', the story of Colin Phillips, a rubbish-tip worker. At the age of 16 Colin decided that what he wanted most in life was a Rolls-Royce. Five years later, after working six days a week on a rubbish tip, he became the proud owner of an elegant blue Silver Shadow. Colin, an example to us all, said, 'It was hard work, but rubbish is all I know.'

* * *

45

'No birds, no booze, no fags, but what a motor!'

When American troops entered Mussolini's headquarters in Rome at the end of the fighting in Italy, among the things they 'liberated' were two Rolls-Royce cars – the property of the Fascist dictator.

*   *   *

Dr Frederick J. Eikerenkoetter II ('Reverend Ike' to his followers), the head of the United Christian Evangelistic Association of America, uses the Rolls-Royce motor car to spread his gospel of brotherly love and charity. When asked about the seeming extravagance, the Rev. replied, 'You must love yourself before you can love anyone else. Anyway Christ rode on the Rolls-Royce of his day – an ass.' He also said in an interview, 'In my church we don't teach poverty. We teach aiming for riches. These damn cars are the nearest thing I've come across to the chariots of the Lord.'

Bhagwan Shree Rajneesh with one of his (at last count)
forty-seven Rolls-Royce cars

Bhagwan Shree Rajneesh off for a ride in the 'tranquility
that compares to the endless peace discovered by the Buddha',
thanks to the remarkable suspension of the Corniche.

Surpassing the Reverend Ike is Bhagwan Shree Rajneesh of the city of Rajneeshpuram, Oregon, USA, and Poona, India. His followers have been showering Rolls-Royce cars on Bhagwan like manna from heaven. Since 1981 they've given him an average of one a month, and at the time of writing he has in trust forty-seven, one of which is bulletproof. A spokesman for the sect explained: 'He likes to go for a drive.' The sect newspaper also said: 'Thanks to the unique suspension on the Rolls-Royce, he rides in a tranquillity that compares with the endless peace discovered by the Buddha.' Bhagwan announced recently: 'There is nothing holy about being poor.'

*   *   *

The Peninsula Hotel, Hong Kong, has a fleet of ten Rolls-Royce motor cars for the use of its guests.

*   *   *

In 1946 four masked men in a Rolls-Royce thundered across the drawbridge of Hever Castle in Kent, home of the Astors, at four in the morning. Ten minutes later they thundered back again, having stolen Ann Boleyn's prayer book, Henry VIII's dagger and twelve other items.

*   *   *

The best shot Texas golfer John Goulds ever played was his four iron on the 180-yard sixteenth at the Greentree Country Club tournament. He sank it in one –and won a Silver Wraith.

*   *   *

Alfred Vanderbilt II was recently reported as selling his Rolls-Royce for an excellent reason: 'Every time I get out of it, everything else seems like an anti-climax.'

*   *   *

The odds on your being an Owner are highest of all if you're an inhabitant of Monaco. Prince Rainier's minuscule country has the highest per capita ownership of Rolls-Royces in the world: one for every 65.1 inhabitants.

At the other extreme, the odds are probably lowest in the People's Republic of China, which last time Rolls-Royce counted had six, giving a ratio of one Rolls-Royce to every 167 million Chinese. (For the Rolls-Royce count in Ulan Bator, see 'Apocrypha'.)

*   *   *

An unnamed Silver Cloud Owner from Cheshire, concerned about constant delays in minor repairs to his car, discovered to his horror that the Nantwich Executive Car Centre had sold his Rolls-Royce 'to ease a cash-flow problem', as the managing director of the company explained. The Owner got £7,000 compensation. The managing director got nine months suspended.

* * *

Gerald, Lord Berners, a composer, had a piano built into the back of his Rolls-Royce.

* * *

Sir Edward Nichol of Littleton Park, Middlesex, bought, entire, King Edward VII's Coronation dressing room at Westminster Abbey. He used it as a garage for his two 1926 Rolls-Royces.

* * *

Lord Baden-Powell's Rolls-Royce was a gift from Scouts, Cubs, Guides and Brownies, each of whom contributed one penny to the magnificent gift.

* * *

In 1962 92-year-old millionaire Gilbert Beale, head of Carter's Tested Seeds, drove his Rolls-Royce and three passengers into the River Thames at Pangbourne. He was rescued within minutes. Witnesses said that although the passengers were terrified, the imperturbable nonegenarian remained calm throughout his ordeal.

* * *

Lloyd George, who inherited Lord Kitchener's Rolls-Royce, had a drinks cabinet installed, and later (and possibly as a direct result) a stool to support his gouty leg.

* * *

The world's highest paid pianist, Wladziu Valentino Liberace is currently going on stage at Radio City Music Hall in a silver Rolls-Royce studded with mirrors on the outside. Liberace, the prince of understatement, emerges from his exotic vehicle in a silver sequin suit and a rhinestone-embroidered blue fox cloak with a 16-foot train. His chauffeur, Terry, also wears sequined white livery.

* * *

Probably the loudest Rolls-Royce was the Phantom II belonging to record breaker Sir Malcolm Campbell. It carried not only a Klaxon horn and a Bosch horn, but also a particularly loud siren, which he used to announce his arrival at racing meets. For much more about the illustrious Sir Malcolm see *The Heroes*.

*   *   *

Lord Louis Mountbatten owned several Rolls-Royces. The first, a wedding present from his wife, Edwina Ashley of Broadlands, was a 1919 Silver Ghost Barker cabriolet. It previously belonged to Edward, Prince of Wales.

The second was truly historic. Not only was it the world's first car with dipping headlights (a modification devised by his lordship), but it was the first 'modern' looking Rolls-Royce. Mountbatten, with the help of his friend Sir Phillip Sassoon, had the bonnet modified by Barker to give the effect of streamlining. To say Rolls-Royce was aghast at the un-Roycean appearance of the car is to put it mildly. First the company tried to block the sale of the car; then it tried to invalidate the warranty. Eventually, however, as the new car elicited more and more favourable comments, the company withdrew its objections – indeed, from about that time most Rolls-Royces followed the Mountbatten model.

This famous old vehicle has made some recent public appearance; it was used in the BBC's *Forsyte Saga* as the car in which Fleur Forsyte travelled to her wedding; and in 1972 Lord Mountbatten, then President of the Royal Automobile Club, drove it along Pall Mall during the Club's 75th anniversary celebrations.

*   *   *

Lord Mountbatten's third Rolls-Royce also made history in a minor way. It was probably the first automobile to be equipped with swivelling head lamps – a personal Mountbatten modification.

*   *   *

Lord Mountbatten's fourth Rolls-Royce carried a code in the number plate: LM 0246, which, being translated, was London Mayfair 0246, Lord Louis's ex-directory London phone number.

*   *   *

Peter Sellers had number plates PS 199 and PS 1872 on his Rolls-Royces. He made great efforts to acquire PS 1 from a dour Scottish woman, offering first £1,000 and then £2,500. To his extreme annoyance, she refused to sell.

*   *   *

Paul Raymond of Raymond's Revuebar, where young ladies appear clad in little more than a smile, owned FU 2.

*   *   *

A firm of Dorset tea merchants commemorate Vincent You-mans's immortal song hit with T 42.

* * *

Jean Harlow, platinum-blonde film goddess of the 1930s and Rolls-Royce Owner, held that seven was her lucky number. Hence her licence plates: 7R7 777. Unfortunately, she died in 1937.

* * *

The world's best-read romantic novelist, Barbara Cartland, has a Rolls-Royce to match her gorgeous ensembles: it is pink. Miss Cartland's choice of number plate is a reflection of her perennial youthfulness: BC 29.

* * *

The famous pink Rolls-Royce used in *Thunderbirds* (FAB 1), in which the doddering Parker chauffeured Lady Penelope through a hundred thrilling adventures, was, of course, Rolls-Royce approved.

* * *

We are indebted to Noel Woodall of Blackpool – who knows more about car number plates than anyone – for the following British Rolls-Royce plates:

COM	1C	Jimmy Tarbuck
MB	1	Max Bygraves
JOK	IE	Mike Reid
1	LAF	Bernard Manning
BJM	1	Bernard Manning
3	LG	Larry Grayson
HS	92	Harry Secombe
NG	10	Noelle Gordon
R	77	Raymonde (Hairdresser and Derby winner)
EH	1	Engelbert Humperdinck
ERN	1E	Ernest Mainwaring (a Staffordshire business-man)
DOB	1	The Duke of Bedford
1	DOB	The Duke of Bedford
NY	1	Nick Young (of *Tomorrow's World*)
ABC	1	Lord Mayor of Leicester
LM	0	Lord Mayor of London
G	0	Lord Provost of Glasgow
S	0	Lord Provost of Edinburgh
6	IDER	H. P. Bulmer

RU	18	John Steele (of Steele's Wheels)
RRM	1	Rolls-Royce Motors
RR	1	H. R. Owen (Rolls-Royce distributors – they paid a world-record price for it)
3	GXM	Princess Margaret

*   *   *

Towards the end of the Second World War, Churchill and Roosevelt had an important meeting with King Ibn Saud of Saudi Arabia. Churchill had arranged a gift of cutlery; but when Roosevelt offered the King a C-47 aeroplane, Churchill, improvising brilliantly, announced, 'And I should like to offer Your Majesty the finest car in the world.' Within hours surprised executives at Derby were commanded by the PM's office to start on a rush job – a car fit for a king. It was furnished with a semi-circular rear seat on which His Majesty could sit cross-legged; it was fitted with extra-wide running boards for his bodyguards, a siren, searchlights, a copper water tank and sterling silver wash basin and drain, an extra-powerful radio, alabaster thermos flasks, and a built-in cabinet for brushes and combs. The bodywork, leather upholstery and cabinetwork were in a rich dark green.

The King was delighted – but said he'd prefer more conventional seats.

*   *   *

In 1961 Lord Derby was fined £5 for colliding with a halt sign. His defence: that the bonnet of his Rolls-Royce restricted his vision. A spokesman from Rolls-Royce commented huffily: "The visibility is quite satisfactory."

*   *   *

In 1949 92-year-old playwright/philosopher George Bernard Shaw decided that he would like to meet comedian Danny Kaye, then the toast of London. He sent a chauffeur-driven Rolls-Royce for Danny, and they took tea together at Shaw's home in Ayot St Lawrence. On the return journey the Rolls-Royce crashed and Danny ended a memorable day in the Middlesex Hospital.

*   *   *

The first British royal Owner was the Duke of Windsor who, attracted to the car after his adventures in the First World War, drove a Silver Ghost.

*   *   *

King George V disliked motor cars in general because they normally involved stooping to get in. His sister Princess Victoria gave him his first ride in a Rolls-Royce at Sandringham. After a few miles the monarch emerged, commenting, 'Just like getting out of a rabbit hutch.'

*　　*　　*

The Duke of Edinburgh was lent a very special car by Rolls-Royce: a Bentley prototype of the Phantom IV with the new, and enormously powerful straight-eight engine. The Duke could – and did – drive it at 130 m.p.h. Hence its nickname: the 'Scalded Cat'.

*　　*　　*

For fifty years the official Royal motor car was a Daimler, not a Rolls-Royce. The first monarch to break with this tradition was Her Majesty The Queen. As the Princess Elizabeth, she and the Duke of Edinburgh were to be given a new Daimler as a wedding present from the Royal Air Force. The happy couple expressed a preference for the Phantom IV – and so a Royal Rolls-Royce tradition began.

*　　*　　*

The Phantom IV was almost 19 feet long and 6 feet high. (Legend has it that the minimum distance for British parking meters was established to accommodate it.) It had two special-edition instruction books which have since become rare collector's items: one in grey leather with red and gold lettering for the front seat, and a de luxe version bound in white leather for the rear seat.

*　　*　　*

The Rolls-Royce Phantom IV was an extremely limited edition: 'For Royal personages and heads of state only.' Only eighteen were produced.

*　　*　　*

The list of first Owners of the Phantom IV is certainly the most impressive for any model of any car ever made. Here it is in its entirety:

Princess Elizabeth and the Duke of Edinburgh
Rolls-Royce Motors
The Shah of Iran (two)
The Sheikh of Kuwait (three)
The Duke of Gloucester
The Duchess of Kent
Generalissimo Franco (three)

Prince Aga Khan
Prince Talal al Saud Ryal of Saudi Arabia
King Feisal II
The Prince Regent of Iraq
Queen Elizabeth II
Princess Margaret

*   *   *

The Shah of Iran must have been one of the best customers Rolls-Royce ever had. His astonishing collection included virtually every model of Rolls-Royce ever made, from the Silver Ghost to the Silver Shadow. It included a Phantom I, II, III, IV (two), V and VI, a Twenty, a 20/25, a 25/30, the first left-hand drive Camargue ever delivered and a blue Corniche.

*   *   *

In October 1971, to celebrate the 2,500th anniversary of the Persian Empire, the Shah threw the ritziest party of modern, and possibly all, times. The guest list read like the *Statesman's Year-book* – nine kings, five queens, sixteen presidents, two sultans, an emperor (Haile Selassie, who brought his diamond-encrusted chihuahua, Chicheebee) not to mention Marshal Tito, Princess Grace, Prince Rainier and, anticlimactically, Spiro T. Agnew. To accommodate this 160-acre superthrash, the Shah had sixty-one air-conditioned, Persian-carpeted tents erected and brought in (largely from Maxim's of Paris) 165 chefs, 7,700 pounds of meat, half a ton of fresh cream and, confounding rumours that it was a bring-your-own-bottle affair, 25,000 bottles of vintage wine (i.e., 50 per guest). An army of hairdressers, 300 wigs, and 240 pounds of hairpins took care of the guests' hairstyles. And guess what kind of cars ferried the pleasure seekers from tent to tent? No, not Dafs.

*   *   *

The Shah may have started a fashion. In March 1984 at what *The Times* called 'the party to end all parties', the Sultan of Brunei threw a 4,000-guest, 350-acre bash to celebrate Brunei's independence. Once again kings, princes, sultans and other heads of state jostled amid scenes of *Arabian Nights* luxury. And once again every senior foreign visitor was given personal use of a Rolls-Royce – from the Sultan's own stable of 110 cars. In addition, the Sultan himself appeared in a long-wheelbase six-door Rolls-Royce, specially created for him. As *The Times* put it, he didn't have to ask the price: the sultanate's estimated earnings for 1984 were equivalent to about £3 billion sterling.

*   *   *

The longest Rolls-Royce

The Sultan of Brunei's six-door car is the longest Rolls-Royce ever made. He ordered two – one for himself and one for his latest wife. They cost £140,000 each (the price of forty Austin Metros); they're 20 feet 6 inches long; they weigh 2½ tons; and they take twelve weeks to produce. Robert Jankel Design of Weybridge converts them from standard Silver Spur limousines. Each car has six seats, two separate air-conditioning systems (for front and back), colour television, video recorder, cassette player with graphic equalizer and a two-way communication system so that the bulletproof glass between driver and passenger doesn't have to be lowered.

* * *

When the Peacock Throne toppled in 1979, the Shah's Silver Ghost and one Phantom IV were in Britain being serviced by Rolls-Royce. The Ayatollahs lost no time in claiming them, as belonging to the State. Equally swiftly, the Shah's estate laid claim to them. Rolls-Royce (of course) remained neutral. The case is still in litigation. The prize: £200,000 worth of superb motor cars.

* * *

General Franco's three Phantom IVs were all bulletproofed.

* * *

King Farouk of Egypt was also a multiple Owner. When in exile in Rome, he ordered a new Bentley. But by the time it arrived, Farouk (who gave new dimensions to the word self-indulgence) was too fat to get in.

* * *

55

After their fairy-tale wedding, Prince Rainier and Princess Grace of Monaco drove through the streets of the principality in an open Silver Cloud, a gift from the loyal Monégasques.

* * *

On his return from Sir Winston Churchill's funeral, the Duke of Gloucester ordered his chauffeur to let him take the wheel. The Duchess counselled against this. The Duke insisted. Not much later the Rolls-Royce was in a field and the Duchess in hospital with a broken arm.

* * *

Princess Margaret took delivery of a new Rolls-Royce in 1972. But before she would accept it, she insisted that the indicators be removed; that the traditional gloss woodwork be replaced with matt; and that the rear lights be refitted in a cluster.

* * *

The Queen has five official state Rolls-Royces. They are all painted royal claret (a deep red) and black – a tradition going back to the colours of the royal horse-drawn carriages. Indeed, Rippon, the pre-war Rolls-Royce coachbuilder, could claim lineal descent from Walter Rippon, official coachbuilder to Queen Elizabeth I.

The state Rolls-Royces do not carry number plates or tax discs – the only cars in Great Britain allowed this privilege. All of them have a fitting on the front of the roof to carry a painted shield of the royal arms and a small royal standard (flown on major ceremonial occasions). Each car carries a small coat of arms on both rear doors. There is also a blue light that can be flashed at night as a warning to the police. There is only one royal ceremonial mascot: a St George and the Dragon in solid silver. It is transferred from car to car as necessary.

* * *

One of the royal Rolls-Royces is second-hand. A Jubilee Landaulette (Phantom IV) was acquired in 1954. The back lets down to make a half-open car.

* * *

The other royal cars are the original Phantom IV (see above), two Phantoms V bought in 1960 and 1961; and the number one royal Rolls-Royce: a very special Phantom VI.

* * *

The royal Phantom VI was a gift. Commissioned for the Queen's Silver Jubilee in 1977 by the British motor industry, it was, ironically, the subject of a twelve-month delay because of an

The Viceroy leaving Dunbar, 1927

Only skin-deep: replica of 1930s Rolls-Royce body
with modern American engine and running gear

industrial dispute at Mulliner Park Ward. But on 29 March 1978 the new car was presented to Her Majesty. It is 19 feet 10 inches long, 6 feet 7 inches wide, 6 feet 1 inch high, and has a turning circle of 52 feet. It weighs just over 3 tons unladen, and its fuel tank holds 23 gallons.

The roof of the car has been raised 4 inches over the Phantom's normal 5 feet 7 inches. The rear compartment is enclosed in clear Perspex for state occasions. When greater privacy is needed, the Perspex 'bubble' is enclosed in a detachable hard-top with a tiny rear window. This is made of sound-proofed aluminium and is normally carried in the boot. (The royal boot very rarely carries luggage.) Even greater privacy is provided by screens fitted to the rear quarter windows (and also carried in the boot).

When not carrying the Queen (and therefore the St George mascot), the royal Phantom has a kneeling Silver Lady.

The royal bumpers are specially designed to be removable, reducing the car's length to a handy 19 feet 1 inch – which neatly fits the garage on the royal yacht, *Britannia*.

Garaging when on tour is provided by the police, who take care of the great car on overnight stays.

Usually, the royal Phantoms have had grey West of England cloth upholstery. For the Phantom VI the colour was changed to Baroda blue – a very pale blue. There are matching Wilton carpets and lambswool rugs.

Unlike other Phantoms, the royal Rolls-Royce carries no television set, no cocktail cabinet in the rear compartment. Instead there is a veneered cassette holder (with tapes of music by the band of the Brigade of Guards). Above this is an Asprey clock, and in the extra-wide central arm rest a Philips pocket dictation machine, a radio cassette player and a large mirror on a swivel. Extra vents for refrigerated cold air at head height are unique to the royal car – in sunny weather the Perspex dome can make the rear compartment like an oven.

The rear seat elevates $3\frac{1}{2}$ inches so that we can get a better view of Her Majesty on state occasions. She always sits directly behind the driver (normally Mr Harrison, senior royal chauffeur), while Prince Philip sits on her left behind a detective. Interestingly, Mulliner Park Ward made the seats on the Queen's side softer than those on Prince Philip's. Another non-standard feature – the running boards. They're smooth instead of having the normal ribbed-rubber finish so that the Queen doesn't catch her heel when alighting.

The gear most often used in a royal Phantom is second. This is the gear used for travel in state processions.

Official government fuel consumption figures for the royal

The Prince of Wales
Tour of India, 1922

Phantom are 9.6 m.p.g. in town traffic and 15.0 m.p.g. at a constant 56 m.p.h.

* * *

All the royal Rolls-Royces are maintained at the Royal Mews, Buckingham Palace, in the charge of the Crown Equerry, Lieutenant-Colonel Sir John Miller, KCVO, DSO, MC. Daily washing is the rule. This is carried out by an old-fashioned method, bucket and chamois leather, rather than more vigorous techniques that might jeopardize the exquisite paintwork.

* * *

Only one American president, Woodrow Wilson, is known for certain to have owned anything as un-American as a Rolls-Royce. Wilson's car was a gift from his friends just before he died – a handsome Oxford tourer in his Princeton colours. There are, however, unconfirmed reports that in the 1930s F. D. Roosevelt acquired a second-hand 1925 Canterbury limousine, formerly the property of Mrs M. E. Cady. And Ulysses S. Grant IV – presumably a descendant of the President – owned a Springfield Rolls-Royce.

Ronald Reagan, even in his movie-star days, made do with a Cadillac.

* * *

Nobel prize winners who were also Owners:

Guglielmo Marconi (Physics)
Rudyard Kipling (Literature)
George Bernard Shaw (Literature)
Ernest Hemingway (Literature)
Woodrow Wilson (Peace)
and Alfred Nobel himself.

*   *   *

The fifteen best quotes by or about Owners:

I believe the power to make money is a gift of God.
John D. Rockefeller

The saddest thing I can imagine is to get used to luxury.
Charles Chaplin

I've been rich and I've been poor. Rich is better.
Richard Usmar (originally said by Sophie Tucker)

A man who has a million dollars is as well off as if he were rich.
John Jacob Astor

Don't kick a man unless he's down.
Horatio Bottomley

One can never be too thin or too rich.
The Duchess of Windsor

I'm as pure as the driven slush.
Tallulah Bankhead

I don't know how much money I've got. . . . I did ask the accountant how much it came to. I wrote it down on a bit of paper. But I've lost the bit of paper.
John Lennon

There will soon be only five kings left: the king of spades, the king of diamonds, the king of clubs, the king of hearts and the king of England.
King Farouk of Egypt

The weak shall inherit the earth – but not the mineral rights.
John Paul Getty

Try everything once except incest and folk dancing.
Sir Thomas Beecham

I have a lust for diamonds, almost like a disease.
Elizabeth Taylor

She has a Rolls-Royce body and a Balham mind.
Beachcomber

Money is God in action.
Frederick J. Eikerenkoetter II (Reverend Ike)

If, however, he [the English gentleman] happens to have been left one [a Rolls-Royce] by an eccentric aunt, it should be very old and not very clean. Some gentlemen carry this further, keeping old sacks on the back seat, and leaving bird messes on the roof where the chickens have roosted.
Donald Sutherland; *The English Gentleman*

The List

Who wants to be a millionaire? I don't.

Cole Porter

Here is a list of famous Owners, in no particular order. It is certainly not totally comprehensive, but it is probably the longest such list ever compiled. Readers may like to test their general knowledge by identifying them all. To start you off:

Hoot Gibson rivalled Tom Mix as King of the Cowboys. He made and lost and made another fortune in movies. And he had two Rolls-Royces.

Michael Arlen had a *succès de scandale* with his novel *The Green Hat* in the 1920s. Rebecca West described him as every other inch a gentleman. He had a yellow Rolls-Royce (and a green carnation).

Sax Rohmer, novelist, created Dr Fu Manchu – the original sinister Oriental.

Sir Banister Fletcher wrote the ever-popular *A History of Architecture on the Comparative Method*.

Josef von Sternberg was the man who guided Marlene Dietrich to stardom. And in 1930 he provided her with a Rolls-Royce.

Prince Birabongse of Siam (Thailand), better known as Bira, was a highly successful racing driver between the wars.

Harry Cohn was the most feared man in Hollywood. He ran Columbia Pictures with an iron fist and said to reporters (truthfully): 'I don't get ulcers. I give 'em.'

61

And Perle Mesta ('the hostess with the mostest') was the US ambassadress and party-giver on whom the musical *Call Me Madam* was based.

Vladimir Ilich Lenin
Guglielmo Marconi
George Bernard Shaw
Elvis Presley
David Lloyd George
Sir Edwin Lutyens
Sir Banister Fletcher
Prince Birabongse of Siam
Gracie Fields
Sir Billy Butlin
The King of Serbia
Henry Curtis-Bennet, KC
Douglas Fairbanks
Pierre Michelin
Howard Hawks
Sir Frederick Henry Royce
Michael Caine
Ernest Hemingway
Claude Johnson
Lord Dacre (Hugh Trevor-Roper)
Vladimir Horowitz
Mae West
Baron Edouard de Rothschild
The Nizam of Hyderabad
W. R. Vanderbilt
The Maharaja of Mysore
Jimmy Tarbuck
Sir Jesse Boot
J. Arthur Rank
Lord Kitchener
Barbra Streisand
Tommy Sopwith
King Carol of Romania
Lord Beaverbrook
Dudley Moore
Sir Malcolm Campbell
J. Pierpont Morgan
Roberto Rossellini
The Marquis of Crewe
Larry Grayson
Emperor Haile Selassie
The Maharaja of Cooch Behar

The People's Republic of China
  (unknown purchaser)
General Franco
Max Bygraves
Gary Cooper
The Third Duke of Westminster
Nubar Gulbenkian
Alfred Bird
Sir John French
Lord Fisher
The Marquis of Exeter
Prince Aly Khan
Lord Birkenhead
Lord Baden-Powell
Gene Hackman
Edgar Wallace
Idi Amin
W. D. Wills
R. D.'Oyly Carte
The Lieutenant-General His
  Highness Farzand-i-Khas-
  i-Daulat-i-Inglishia,
  Mansur-i-Zaman, Amir-
  ul-Umra, Maharaja Dhiraj
  Raj Rajeshwar Shree,
  Maharaja-i-Rajgan, Maha-
  raja Sir Bhupindra Singh,
  Mohinder Bahadur, Yadu
  Vanshavatans Bhatti
  Kul Bhushan, Maharaja
  Dhiraj of Patalia,
  GCSI, GCIE, GCVO, GBE
Jack Warner
President Samora Machel
  of Mozambique
S. Gestetner
Pola Negri
Sax Rohmer
Sir Terence Rattigan
Cary Grant
W. Somerset Maugham
Prince Alexis Mldvani

Peter Sellers
Eddie Fisher
Marshal Tito
Aristotle Onassis
Greta Garbo
Lawrence of Arabia
President Woodrow Wilson
Marie, Dowager Empress
 of Russia
Zsa Zsa Gabor
Hoot Gibson
John Conteh
Tallulah Bankhead
The Maharaj Ji
King George of Greece
Adolph Zukor
Red Skelton
The Duke of Bedford
George Jessel
Brian Epstein
J. D. Rockefeller
Yul Brynner
Zeppo Marx
George Harrison
Letitia Overend
Carl Laemmle
Engelbert Humperdinck
Gerry della Femina
Rod la Rocque
Jackie Coogan
Marilyn Miller
J. Ringling
Paul McCartney
Sir Johnson Forbes Robertson
Barbara Cartland
S. J. Bloomingdale
Hugh Hefner
Sid Grauman
The Emperor Yoshihito
 of Japan
Sir Arnold Weinstock
Richard Burton
Gordon Selfridge
George Eyston
Sir Oswald Mosley
Cole Porter

Sir Ralph Richardson
The Kabaka of Buganda
Princess Marina
Barry Sheene
Diana Dors
Emperor Hirohito
The Duke of Kent
G. Pabst
The Reverend Ike
Anita Loos
Alfred Nobel
Billy Wilder
Sammy Davis Jr
Isaac Stern
Lord Montagu of Beaulieu
Joseph von Sternberg
Marlene Dietrich
Mack Sennett
Perle Mesta
Adnan Khashoggi
Howard Hughes
Jack Dempsey
Victor Lownes
Gloria Swanson
Irving Berlin
Al Jolson
Sam Spiegel
Richard Harris
Darryl Zanuck
Jean Harlow
Tommy Manville Jr
Andrew Mellon
Clara Bow
Bhagwan Shree Rajneesh
Joseph Pulitzer
Mike Todd
Lew Grade
Princess Grace of Monaco
Bernard Buffet
Ben Lyon
Georges Mathieu
Deborah Kerr
Rex Harrison
William Holden
Lerner and Loewe
Dick Emery

John Jacob Astor
Mike Yarwood
Prince Rainier
Elizabeth Taylor
Peter de Savary
Jimmy Savile
Norma Talmadge
Michael Arlen
The Warner Brothers
The Duke of Windsor
Brigitte Bardot
Roger Moore
Harry Cohn
Princess Margaret
Keith Moon
J. B. Duke
John Ford
Jody Scheckter
F. N. Doubleday
A. Bulova
The Duke of Gloucester
Irving Thalberg
Sir Gordon Richards
Gypsy Rose Lee
The Ayatollah Khomeini
Harold Lloyd
Kaye Don
Max Wall
Fred Karno
J. D. Rockefeller
The Shah of Persia
Nancy, Lady Astor
Benito Mussolini
Eamon de Valera
Rikidozan
Leonid Brezhnev
Henry Ford
Fred Astaire
Neville Chamberlain
Sheik Ahmed Yamani
Tsar Nicholas II
Rudyard Kipling
Paris Singer
Viscount Montgomery
   of Alamein
Sir Charles Chaplin

Luigi Innocenti
Sir Ernest Tate
Admiral of the Fleet Lord Beatty
Jack Benny
The Aga Khan
Viscount Curzon
Rudolph Valentino
Horatio Bottomley
General Foch
Air Marshal Lord Trenchard
William Randolph Hearst
Prince Alexis Orloff
General Sir Douglas Haig
Ivor Novello
Georges Clemenceau
George Formby
Coco Chanel
Tony Jacklin
Prince Chula Chakrabongse
Larry Flynt
Tom Mix
David Ogilvy
Harley Granville-Barker
Pearl White
Sir Thomas Lipton
General George Patton
The Hon. Dorothy Paget
Mary Pickford
Lord Beaverbrook
Sir John Moores
Harry Secombe
Jomo Kenyatta
Adele Astaire
General Sikorski of Poland
Gertrude Lawrence
Dame Nellie Melba
King Farouk of Egypt
Jack Buchanan
The Hon. Charles Rolls
The Sultan of Brunei
Doctor Warre
The King of Afghanistan
Raymonde
Sir John Ellerman
Noelle Gordon
A. J. Cronin

Lewis J. Selznick
Lord Northcliffe
Sir Montague Burton
F. Scott Fitzgerald
Thakor Sahib of Rajkote
King Constantine of Greece
Reginald J. Mitchell
Afred Dunhill
Herbert Austin
Muhammad Ali
Sir Harry Lauder
The Queen Mothers of Nepal
John Lennon
King Ibn Saud
S. H. Grylls
Lady Docker
Brian Jones

Emil Savundra
Raymond Chandler
Sir Emsley Carr
Bernard Manning
General Joffre
Gary Glitter
Lord Dunsany
Sir Henry Segrave
Earl Mountbatten of Burma
Georges Simenon
Queen Wilhelmina of
    The Netherlands
Sir Thomas Beecham
P. G. Wodehouse
and, of course, Her Majesty
    Queen Elizabeth II

The Rolls-Royce Silver Cloud—$13,550.

"At 60 miles an hour the loudest noise in this new Rolls-Royce comes from the electric clock"

What __makes__ Rolls-Royce the best car in the world? "There is really no magic about it—
it is merely patient attention to detail," says an eminent Rolls-Royce engineer.

1. "At 60 miles an hour the loudest noise comes from the electric clock," reports the Technical Editor of THE MOTOR. The silence of the engine is uncanny. Three mufflers tune out sound frequencies—acoustically.

2. Every Rolls-Royce engine is run for seven hours at full throttle before installation, and each car is test-driven for hundreds of miles over varying road surfaces.

3. The Rolls-Royce is designed as an *owner-driven* car. It is eighteen inches shorter than the largest domestic cars.

4. The car has power steering, power brakes and automatic gear-shift. It is very easy to drive and to park. No chauffeur required.

5. There is no metal-to-metal contact between the body of the car and the chassis frame—except for the speedometer drive. The entire body is insulated and under-sealed.

6. The finished car spends a week in the final test-shop, being fine-tuned. Here it is subjected to ninety-eight separate ordeals. For example, the engineers use a stethoscope to listen for axle-whine.

7. The Rolls-Royce is guaranteed for three years. With a new network of dealers and parts-depots from Coast to Coast, service is no longer any problem.

8. The famous Rolls-Royce radiator has never been changed, except that when Sir Henry Royce died in 1933 the monogram RR was changed from red to black.

9. The coachwork is given five coats of primer paint, and hand rubbed between each coat, before fourteen coats of finishing paint go on.

10. By moving a switch on the steering column, you can adjust the shock-absorbers to suit road conditions. (The lack of fatigue in driving this car is remarkable.)

11. Another switch defrosts the rear window, by heating a network of 1360 invisible wires in the glass. There are two separate ventilating systems, so that you can ride in comfort with all the windows closed. Air conditioning is optional.

12. The seats are upholstered with eight hides of English leather—enough to make 128 pairs of soft shoes.

13. A picnic table, veneered in French walnut, slides out from under the dash. Two more swing out behind the front seats.

14. You can get such optional extras as an Espresso coffee-making machine, a dictating machine, a bed, hot and cold water for washing, an electric razor.

15. You can lubricate the entire chassis by simply pushing a pedal from the driver's seat. A gauge on the dash shows the level of oil in the crankcase.

16. Gasoline consumption is remarkably low and there is no need to use premium gas; a happy economy.

17. There are two separate systems of power brakes, hydraulic and mechanical. The Rolls-Royce is a very safe car—and also a very lively car. It cruises serenely at eighty-five. Top speed is in excess of 100 m.p.h.

18. Rolls-Royce engineers make periodic visits to inspect owners' motor cars and advise on service.

ROLLS-ROYCE AND BENTLEY

19. The Bentley is made by Rolls-Royce. Except for the radiators, they are identical motor cars, manufactured by the same engineers in the same works. The Bentley costs $300 less, because its radiator is simpler to make. People who feel diffident about driving a Rolls-Royce can buy a Bentley.

PRICE. The car illustrated in this advertisement—f.o.b. principal port of entry—costs **$13,550.**

If you would like the rewarding experience of driving a Rolls-Royce or Bentley, get in touch with our dealer. His name is on the bottom of this page: Rolls-Royce Inc., 10 Rockefeller Plaza, New York, N.Y.

JET ENGINES AND THE FUTURE

Certain airlines have chosen Rolls-Royce turbo-jets for their Boeing 707's and Douglas DC8's. Rolls-Royce prop-jets are in the Vickers Viscount, the Fairchild F-27 and the Grumman Gulfstream.

Rolls-Royce engines power more than half the turbo-jet and prop-jet airliners supplied to us on order for world airlines.

Rolls-Royce now employ 42,000 people and the company's engineering experience does not stop at motor cars and jet engines. These are Rolls-Royce diesel and gasoline engines for many other applications.

The huge research and development resources of the company are now at work on many projects for the future, including nuclear and rocket propulsion.

Special showing of the Rolls-Royce and Bentley at Salter Automotive Imports, Inc., 9009 Carnegie Ave., tomorrow through April 26.

 *The Car*

If you have to ask the price, you can't afford it.

J. Pierpont Morgan

The most famous
Rolls-Royce advertisement
of all time

The factory where the first Royce car was made:
Cooke Street, Manchester

The Car

The best car in the world? Says who?

Well, a motoring journalist first said it in 1908 and even though there have been faster cars, better-handling cars and, by its own admission, more comfortable cars, Rolls-Royce has managed to hold on to the title without any obvious or ungentlemanly exertion ever since.

Clever public relations you might think; and true, Claude Johnson, a founder partner of Rolls-Royce, definitely had a genius for publicity, but even he couldn't have done what he did without some terrific basic material.

It was Johnson's idea to turn the first 40/50 into the Silver Ghost by making a body for it out of polished aluminium and silver plating its accessories in time for its first appearance at the 1906 London Motor Show.

It was Johnson's idea to put the same car through the marathon test that set up Rolls-Royce's reputation once and for all. But it wouldn't have been much of a stunt if the car hadn't run without a murmur for 14,371 miles, doubling the world endurance record.

Rolls-Royce hasn't always made perfect cars, but it's always made cars amazing enough to bear the weight of the legends they inspired: the truth about Rolls-Royce cars is often more unlikely than the myths. It is true that every Rolls-Royce radiator is signed on the back by the man who made it; it is true that a Rolls-Royce drove all the way from London to Edinburgh in top gear and repeated the feat 66 years later; it is true that the hydraulic tappets on a Rolls-Royce engine are put together while immersed in paraffin.

Take away the glamour and the great names from Rolls-Royce and you're left with a car with four wheels and an engine like any other. Except that there isn't any other car likely to have an engine whose internals have been polished with finely ground oat husks or wheels with hubs hand painted on a potter's wheel to the Owner's personal specification.

*   *   *

It is possible that Rolls-Royce Motors is the best-known British company name in the world. Letters have been received from remote corners of the world addressed to: 'The Royal Family, care of Rolls-Royce, England.'

*   *   *

An American motoring journalist once described the Rolls-Royce as being 'like the Englishmen who make it, ancient, square, strong and dependable'.

*   *   *

General Motors produce 100,000 cars approximately every three days. In the whole of their eighty-year history, Rolls-Royce has produced about 85,000.

*   *   *

The locks on the 1984 Silver Spirit are made according to a principle first used on the tombs of the Pharaohs, four thousand years ago.

*   *   *

No one is certain who designed the Rolls-Royce radiator grille or the interlinked RR badge.

*   *   *

Every year Rolls-Royce Motors uses enough walnut veneer to cover a full-size soccer pitch.

*   *   *

The pattern of the veneer on one side of the fascia of a modern Rolls-Royce is an exact mirror image of the pattern on the other side.

*   *   *

On the back of the veneer in any Rolls-Royce is a serial number which enables it to be matched up with veneer from the same log should it ever be damaged, since a portion of each is kept in storage at the factory.

*   *   *

An off-the-cuff remark by the great wit F. E. Smith (later Lord Birkenhead) is probably as neat as any slogan ever thought up for Rolls-Royce by an advertising agency:

> Ford and the world Fords with you,
> Rolls and you roll alone.

*   *   *

Even Rolls-Royce makes mistakes. During one test an experimental Phantom chassis flexed so much that its front wheels touched the ground only every 11 feet or so.

*   *   *

Henry Ford's Bentley
on its way to the USA

Rolls-Royce . . . even their mistakes are beautifully made.

D. B. Tubbs

*   *   *

The man who goes to Pooles for his clothes, Purdeys for his guns
and Hardys for his rods goes to Rolls-Royce for his car.

Copy from an early advertisement

*   *   *

Rush hour in Jeddah? The main road to Dover when Labour get in again?
Shree Bhagwan Rajneesh taking a few friends for a drive? (see page 73)

Any Car Can Crawl

Remember the
Remarkable
Record of the 20 h.p.
Rolls-
Royce in
Rushing up the steepest
Roof-like hills
Recommended by
Readers of *Motor* in selected gear
Ratios which at 1,000
Revs of the motor per minute give
15 m.p.h. in lower gear + 50 m.p.h. in higher gear?

Please write for trial run to C. S. Rolls.

1906 advertisement copy

*   *   *

The most expensive advertising photograph in history was taken for Rolls-Royce in 1975. It involved 104 Rolls-Royce cars lined up on an unopened stretch of the M4. The cost of these 'props' at current prices: six million pounds. The art director was John Simeoni; the photographer, Eric Swaine.

Six extra Rolls-Royces were employed to take the drivers (Rolls-Royce distributors) 5 miles to the nearest lavatory.

*   *   *

The finish of the prototype Continental Phantom II was metallic saxe blue, produced by overlaying the paint with a lacquer containing finely ground herring scales.

*   *   *

The same road sign greets motorists on all approach roads to Crewe:

The Borough of Crewe & Nantwich
Home of the best car in the world

*   *   *

Before the days of artificially controlled temperature and humidity the final varnishing of a Rolls-Royce's paintwork could be done only on days when the weather conditions were perfect – approximately one day in every four.

*   *   *

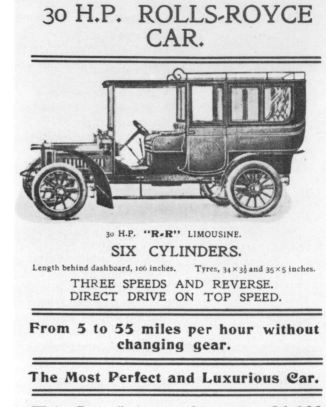

30 H.P. ROLLS-ROYCE CAR.

30 H.P. **"R-R"** LIMOUSINE.

SIX CYLINDERS.

Length behind dashboard, 106 inches.   Tyres, 34 × 3½ and 35 × 5 inches.

THREE SPEEDS AND REVERSE.
DIRECT DRIVE ON TOP SPEED.

From 5 to 55 miles per hour without changing gear.

The Most Perfect and Luxurious Car.

With "Barker" six-seated Limousine - **£1,000**
With "Barker" side-entrance Tonneau   **£890**

Two pages from . . .

All the glass in a modern Rolls-Royce is polished with pumice of a grade normally reserved for the finishing of optical lenses.

*   *   *

The sand used in the casting of Rolls-Royce crank cases is all from the same quarry – Withington sand quarry, near Congleton, Cheshire – the only place in the world which produces the uniquely consistent and pure variety of sand required.

*   *   *

All makers of luxury cars like to boast about their after-sales service. Only Rolls-Royce goes to the extent of running a permanent school for chauffeurs.

On completing a course at the Rolls-Royce chauffeurs' school

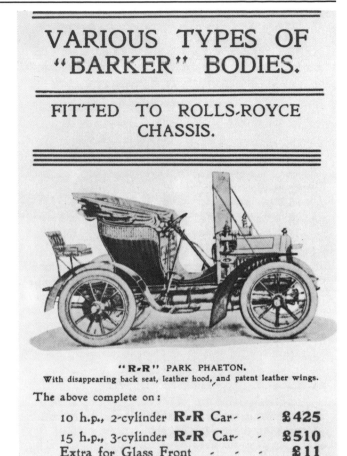

VARIOUS TYPES OF "BARKER" BODIES.

FITTED TO ROLLS-ROYCE CHASSIS.

" R∘R " PARK PHAETON.
With disappearing back seat, leather hood, and patent leather wings.

The above complete on:

10 h.p., 2-cylinder **R∘R** Car- - **£425**
15 h.p., 3-cylinder **R∘R** Car- - **£510**
Extra for Glass Front - - - **£11**

. . . the 1905 Brochure

a driver at first gets only a letter stating he has attended successfully. The ultimate qualification – the cap badge and certificate – comes later, after the pupil has driven more than 30,000 miles in a Rolls-Royce or Bentley or been in sole charge of one for three years. That is not all. After exceeding the required number of miles or years, the applicant must then submit his car to Rolls-Royce Motors for inspection and prove that he has driven that particular car for at least 10,000 miles.

*   *   *

Each stainless-steel wheel disc incorporates a 'picture plate' that is hand-painted on a potter's wheel.

*   *   *

Trade in your Mini Metro
for the air conditioning
on a Silver Spirit.
They cost about the same

For the 5-year-old who has everything: Rolls-Royce has given its blessing to what is probably the world's most desirable Christmas present – a 4-foot-long battery-powered Rolls-Royce Corniche with electronic controls for indicators, hazard-warning lights, horn and headlights. Such noise as is needed to make the car as authentic as possible while it glides along comes from a hidden loudspeaker. It costs around £250, or £140 if you make do with a pedal-driven model.

                    *   *   *

The final polishing of some engine and gearbox parts was done at one time with fine-ground oak husks, jeweller's rouge being too coarse for the job.

                    *   *   *

The air conditioning in a Rolls-Royce costs as much to make as a complete Mini Metro. It changes the air three times a minute.

                    *   *   *

Before the rectangular Rolls-Royce badge was designed the grille carried an oval logo, within which were the words 'The Rolls-Royce radiator'.

                    *   *   *

David Ogilvy's famous 1950s headline: 'At 60 m.p.h. the loudest noise in the new Rolls-Royce comes from the electric clock' was not a new thought. The *Autocar* review of the Silver Ghost in 1907 reads: 'At whatever speed the car is driven, the auditory nerves when driving are troubled by no fuller sound than emanates from an 8-day clock.'

                    *   *   *

In construction every Rolls-Royce is accompanied by a 'history book' which is signed in turn by each of the craftsmen who work on it.

*   *   *

One early Rolls-Royce chauffeur used to drive his car through a pond to cool the brakes at the end of a long descent. This habit had stayed with him from his previous job – driving a coach and four.

*   *   *

Even today, every Rolls-Royce engine is completely hand-built.

*   *   *

In the 1920s and 1930s most Rolls-Royce motor cars were road-tested in France because the roads were faster than in England and the French police more 'co-operative'.

*   *   *

In 1977 sixty-six years after Ernest Hives had driven a Phantom locked in top gear from London to Edinburgh the same car was driven from Edinburgh to London, again in top gear all the way. Even though the car was capable of nearly 80 m.p.h., Hives's average speed in 1911 was only 19.59 m.p.h. The average speed for the more recent run was 35.8 m.p.h.

*   *   *

All Spirit of Ecstasy mascots on Rolls-Royces up to 1951 are signed by Charles Sykes, the artist who made the original sculpture on which the mascots are modelled.

*   *   *

Perhaps the best-ever description of the Rolls-Royce engine was provided by a Mr Paddon (whose claim to fame was that he was the first man to put the characteristic vertical shutters on the Rolls-Royce radiator): 'The great thing about the Rolls-Royce ... is that the engine never gives the impression of turning round. Bloody great pistons in bloody great cylinders going up and down like bloody great lifts.'

*   *   *

One of Rolls-Royce's few wholly unsuccessful ideas was a 1905 model with the stylish name of the Legalimit. Although it had a V8 3.5-litre engine, it was designed to be incapable of exceeding the legal speed limit of 20 m.p.h. Only one was ever sold – to Sir Alfred Harmsworth, the press baron.

*   *   *

AT THE RITZ HOTEL.

People who will have "The Best of Everything" will have Rolls-Royce Cars.

SHOPPING AT "THE MAISON LEWIS."

People who will have "The Best of Everything" will have Rolls-Royce Cars

Overt snobbery from an early advertising campaign

One of the most peculiar
Rolls-Royces of all time,
a Silver Ghost with a
skiff body. It doesn't float

When Rolls-Royce cars were first exported to America they were so quiet that the licensing authorities refused to believe that they were petrol-driven cars, thinking that they must be electrically powered.

*   *   *

The American magazine *Antique Automobile* reported that in the early 1960s a vintage Rolls-Royce was discovered in a deep lake near Chicago. It had been dumped there after a gangland killing. A nickel-plated revolver was found under the front seat.

*   *   *

On Friday, 23 January 1976, the American TV quiz game *High Rollers* featured a Tournament of Champions with the prize of a brand-new Silver Shadow. The producers of the show said they chose the car because they considered it 'the ultimate, the best of all grand prizes'.

After a sudden-death play-off the car was won on the throw of a dice by Carole Vico of Buffalo.

Blankety Blank producers, please note.

*   *   *

New Rolls-Royce models are always subjected to criticism by the diehards. The 20 h.p. Rolls-Royce, one of the most successful models ever, was described by one J. T. C. Moore-Brabazon in a motoring magazine shortly after its launch as 'a very excellent vehicle of a somewhat uninteresting American type'.

*   *   *

The current record mileage for a Rolls-Royce is held by a 1922 20 h.p. owned by an Australian, Mr David Davies. It has over 700,000 miles on the clock.

*   *   *

'You need never change gear in a Rolls-Royce' was a common, and understandable, pre-war saying. The top-gear flexibility of early Rolls-Royces was legendary. Many Rolls-Royce Owners only ever changed gear when they came up against a gradient of Alpine proportions. One woman drove her Rolls-Royce in top for twenty-five years because she was quite incapable of changing gear.

*   *   *

Even the royal family's chauffeurs come to Rolls-Royce Motors for tuition. They take away with them the *Rolls-Royce Chauffeur's Guide* which, among other things, contains many useful hints about the correct way to handle 'royal personages'. 'Remove your cap directly the royal personage appears,' says the book. 'The cap should then remain off until you start your journey.'

*   *   *

Many rather extreme attempts were made to increase the power of the engine in the 3-ton Phantom I. One car had an Amherst Villiers Supercharger driven by an Austin Seven engine tucked in under the bonnet beside the Rolls-Royce engine.

*   *   *

Early Rolls-Royce cars had wooden wheels which creaked when the wood dried out and shrank. Chauffeurs were advised to douse them with water to stop the noise.

*   *   *

Rolls-Royce did not make a complete car until after the Second World War. Before that they made only chassis, the bodies being added by outside coachbuilders.

*   *   *

Up until 1958 the radiator vanes on Rolls-Royce cars opened and shut automatically by thermostat to control the cooling requirements of the engine.

*   *   *

In 1942 nearly every taxi in Blackpool was a Rolls-Royce.

*   *   *

Around 1923 an American soft-drinks manufacturer, the Moxie Company, got hold of a second-hand Silver Ghost, removed the body and had a full-sized replica of a horse mounted on the chassis. A steering column stuck out from the horse's neck at a comfortable reach from the saddle, where the stetson-wearing, six-gun-toting driver sat. Clutch and brake pedals were arranged in the stirrups. No one is quite sure who is responsible, but it is a safe bet that nobody connected with Rolls-Royce had a hand in it. A Rolls-Royce engineer summed up the general reaction: 'Blimey, isn't that a bloody mess?'

The car had a star spot in every important parade in New England for several years, before, presumably, being sent off to the knacker's yard.

*   *   *

In 1955 a visitor to a scrapyard in Edenbridge, Kent, discovered four Silver Ghosts standing on top of each other.

*   *   *

Once a year the Rolls-Royce purchasing director and the factory woodshop superintendent go to Lombardy to buy walnut veneer. They travel incognito, concealing the fact they come from Rolls-Royce, because the mere mention of the name would undoubtedly push the price up.

*   *   *

The first-ever sliding sun roof was made by Henri Labourdette for a Silver·Ghost chassis.

*   *   *

Trainees at the Rolls-Royce Chauffeurs' School are prepared for almost any situation. Not only are they taught what to do in the event of a terrorist attack but also schooled in more traditional skills: 'When opening a door to allow a passenger to get into or out of a car they must touch their hats. They must always get down to open the door to let passengers in or out of a car and must always address customers as "Sir" or "Madam" unless they be titled people, when they must use the proper appellatives – such as to an Archbishop or Duke, "Yes, your Grace", "Your Grace's car is here." To a Baron or Earl, "Yes, my Lord", "Your Lordship's car is waiting."' (From the Rolls-Royce and Bentley Chauffeur's handbook.)

*   *   *

In the 1920s you could buy an American Cadillac with what appeared to be a Rolls-Royce radiator.

*   *   *

In 1976 Rolls-Royce Motors Inc. won a legal action against Custom Cloud Motors Inc. of Florida, which was selling a kit to disguise a Chevrolet Monte-Carlo as a Rolls-Royce.

The customizing kit contained a copy of the radiator grille, a bonnet ornament with a passing resemblance to the Spirit of Ecstasy, rear lights, fibreglass mudguards and a bonnet unit designed to shroud the corresponding part of the Chevrolet. A

Hi Ho Silver! (Ghost)

survey conducted by Rolls-Royce and entered as evidence showed that the so-called Custom Cloud was wrongly identified as a Rolls-Royce by 65 out of 100 Americans.

* * *

In 1953 Rolls-Royce replaced the 4-speed manual gearbox with a General Motors hydraulic gearbox that was essentially the same as the one in a $2,000 Pontiac.

* * *

Some Rolls-Royces were sent to India with blackened windows in the 1920s. They were known as 'purdah wagons'.

* * *

The 1908 Silver Ghost was fitted as standard with an oil-pressure gauge and a gauge to show the air pressure in the petrol tank – but a speedometer would have cost you 15 guineas extra.

* * *

Test drivers on the Silver Spirit clocked up 1 million miles in a year.

* * *

Not any more, they couldn't. Rolls-Royce put a stop to the Custom Cloud with swift legal action

The bodywork on the Corniche is constructed entirely by hand. The car itself takes five months to build.

*   *   *

The company prefers to keep the exact details of what goes on under a Rolls-Royce bonnet to itself. Anyone who has ever asked about the power output of a Rolls-Royce engine has always been given the same polite but discreetly evasive reply: 'Sufficient, sir.'

*   *   *

'Doctors declare the Rolls-Royce to be the only petrol car they could bring up to a patient's house and drive away without the possibility of disturbing the patient.' (Rolls-Royce advertisement, 1910.)

*   *   *

More than six out of ten of all the Rolls-Royces ever built are still on the road.

*   *   *

The camshaft gears of the Phantom were first machined, then hardened, then stoned by hand to make sure they mated perfectly. This hand work took over eighty hours for each set of gears.

*   *   *

A standard 40/50 h.p. Phantom would accelerate quite comfortably from 3 m.p.h. to 60 m.p.h. in top gear.

*   *   *

The 1924 Silver Ghost had anti-lock, servo-assisted braking, a similar system to that featured in a 1983 car advertising campaign as a major technological advance.

*   *   *

For many years the coils on all Rolls-Royce cars were wound by a Miss Florrie Austin on a home-made machine grafted on to the base of an old Singer treadle sewing machine. This did not occupy all her time: she also engraved Rolls-Royce insignia on hub-caps, control-lever plates and switches, cut the slots for valve-stem cotters and made tea for her workmates at the Manchester factory. For doing all this she was paid the going rate of about 27 shillings a week – just enough to buy a dozen loaves at current prices.

*   *   *

In 1968 Rolls-Royce took a Swiss businessman to court to stop him from selling £245 Rolls-Royce 'conversion kits' designed to give any car the Rolls-Royce look.

*   *   *

The first 10 h.p. Rolls-Royce was sold for £395. Today it is worth over £250,000.

*   *   *

The upholstery of some early Rolls-Royce cars was made from the hides of still-born calves to ensure that the leather would be completely unblemished.

*   *   *

The hides on modern Rolls-Royce cars come largely from remote parts of Scandinavia, where an absence of fence posts and barbed wire means less chance of flawed animal skins.

*   *   *

From 1916 to 1929 Albert C. Barley of Kalamazoo, Michigan, USA, made cars called Roamers, that were cheap imitations of Rolls-Royces.

*   *   *

Most modern car manufacturers have to use three body shells in the standard series of impact tests required by safety legislation. The Silver Spirit body is so strong that only one needs be used for the whole series.

*   *   *

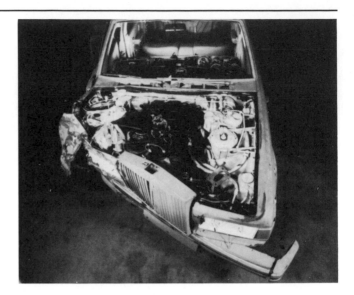

What happens when you drive a £55,000 Rolls-Royce into a block of concrete? Grown men have been known to break down at the sight

The Rolls-Royce name, badge and radiator are in constant need of protection. Every day of the year the company is involved in litigation to prevent their illegal use. The trademarks are covered by 432 registrations in eighty-five countries.

*   *   *

The Birmingham Rolls-Royce dealers, P. J. Evans, recently bought a 67-year-old Silver Ghost with a Thrupp and Maperley body and the first-ever sliding sun-roof. An examination of the engine, which had covered 60,000 miles, showed that the main bearings had worn by only 0.0005 inches and the cast-iron pistons by less than 0.002 inches.

*   *   *

The average family house has around 200 yards of wiring. A Silver Spirit has almost one mile.

*   *   *

Between 1920 and 1931 Rolls-Royce cars were made in America – at Springfield, Massachusetts. Nearly 3,000 Phantoms and Silver Ghosts were produced. But Rolls-Royce never truly adapted to America – for the first three years of production the cars were all right-hand drive – and the desire by Americans for the 'real thing', plus the 1929 Crash, killed off the venture. Some of the most handsome Rolls-Royces produced, however, were made in the USA.

The most famous American coachbuilder of all was Brewster – a direct descendant of one of the Pilgrim Fathers.

*   *   *

An American demonstration Rolls-Royce reaches the point when its driver can remove the 'Running in, please pass' sticker from its rear window and take it for its first major service

No wonder Rolls-Royce USA didn't last. Rolls-Royce would only do things the English way, even in America. For example the American factory *made* a horn button exactly as in England at a cost of $14, when a perfectly adequate one could be bought locally for 75 cents. And the simple push-pull knobs (costing a dollar each) used on all American cars were rejected in favour of a smoother mechanism, the assembly of which involved 227 components and 225 special fasteners. The tools to make it cost $69,000 and the cost per unit was at least twenty times that of the native American product.

*　　*　　*

The most embarrassing moment in Rolls-Royce history: L. J. Belnap, President of Rolls-Royce USA, left the company in April 1925. Rolls-Royce decided to present him with a most expensive engraved Patek Phillipe gold watch in recognition of his services. After a touching speech, the Rolls-Royce Treasurer made to hand over the watch, dropped it – and it was shattered beyond repair.

*　　*　　*

One complete room at the Rolls-Royce factory is mounted on cork: the Standards Room where the calibration of measuring instruments is carried out.

*　　*　　*

A Rolls-Royce apprentice (Peter Wharton who later became chief stylist at Mulliner Park Ward) was once given the job of making a small drawer to be fitted to a car to carry a pack of twenty cigarettes. He was most upset when the complete car was sent back because the drawer did not fit the pack. He had modelled the drawer on the dimensions of a pack of Weights, but the owner smoked Passing Cloud.

*   *   *

A cocktail cabinet with cut-glass decanter is standard equipment on the Phantom VI.

*   *   *

The lines of the Rolls-Royce radiator are slightly bowed to give the appearance of perfect rectilinearity, employing the same principle used by Kallikrates in building the Parthenon. This is known as entasis.

*   *   *

The ball joints in the throttle linkage on the modern Silver Spirit were designed by Sir Henry Royce over fifty years ago. No one has ever been able to improve on them, so they have never been changed.

*   *   *

In 1937 Mr H. E. Symonds picked up a new Phantom III limousine from the Derby factory. Then in fourteen days of driving he covered 5,846 miles (plus 500 at sea) from Derby to Nairobi through blinding storms, sodden marsh and almost impenetrable bush. When he reached Nairobi he turned round and started back across the Sahara Desert and the Atlas Mountains, and returned home 'with every nut about the chassis tight and every wheel true. The Park Ward body was as silent, as dustproof and watertight as at the start of this great journey. And the radiator still required no water since the car left Derby 12,000 miles back.'

*   *   *

The wooden fascia of Rolls-Royce cars is termite-proof.

*   *   *

A happy accident: recent tests have shown that the Spirit of Ecstasy mascot is a near-perfect shape for the deflection of snow from the windscreen.

*   *   *

Every Rolls-Royce craftsman engraves his initials on the back of each radiator he makes.

*   *   *

Across the Sahara and back in thirty-four days (see page 86)

Rolls-Royce armoured cars were built on a standard chassis, but instead of a normal 15-hundredweight body they had to support $3\frac{1}{2}$ tons of $\frac{3}{8}$-inch armour plate. They reached speeds in excess of 70 m.p.h. over desert terrain.

* * *

At the Rolls-Royce factory the cars are always referred to as 'Royces'. They are never, ever, called 'Rollers'.

* * *

Notices have been hung around the factory bearing the legend: 'Beware silent cars.'

* * *

Before the name Silver Ghost was settled on, names for early Rolls-Royces included: Scarlet Pimpernel, Cookie, and Beauty Gal.

* * *

There are five and a half times as many parts in a Rolls-Royce as in the average saloon car.

*   *   *

At the factory two imitation wooden heels are used to test the durability of the Wilton carpet fitted in the cars. The heels rub backwards and forwards 100,000 times over 4 inches of carpet. The factory legend – that the heels were modelled on those of a famous transatlantic film actress – is untrue.

*   *   *

The courtesy lights in the Silver Spirit stay on for 7 seconds after the doors have been closed to allow passengers to settle in their seats. For obvious reasons, this facility is not available on cars exported to countries with a major terrorist problem.

*   *   *

A Rolls-Royce does not break down. It 'fails to proceed'.

*   *   *

Fifty-six yards of Connolly leather piping are used on the carpets and seats in a Rolls-Royce. This is cut from the same Connolly hide as the upholstery.

*   *   *

In the 1920s Klaxon horns on Rolls-Royce cars sent to India were replaced by quieter Bosch horns so as not to scare the sacred cows.

*   *   *

The end of the dipstick on the Rolls-Royce engine is carefully honed to prevent it from scratching the inside of the dipstick tube and thus creating tiny metal shavings that would drop into the engine.

*   *   *

In 1979 on the 75th anniversary of Rolls-Royce the company built seventy-five special cars for each of its three major markets: UK, USA, and 'rest of the world'. Every car had a red rather than black badge on the radiator and a commemorative plaque in the glove-box.

*   *   *

The Rolls-Royce radiator is made entirely by hand and eye – without the aid of measuring instruments.

*   *   *

Examine the coachline that extends the full length of the Silver Spirit. You may be surprised to learn that it is applied by hand. The unerring line is 15 feet 6 inches long.

*   *   *

You will never open the ashtray in a modern Rolls-Royce and find a cigarette end. It empties automatically.

*   *   *

The prototype of the Silver Spirit was test run non-stop for the equivalent of 40,000 miles. When it was stripped down and its components measured for wear they were found to be well within accepted tolerances. 'Nicely run in' was the engineers' verdict.

*   *   *

Driving through France in a Rolls-Royce on their way to visit Royce at his home in Le Canadel, two designers crashed into a horse and cart. A few minutes later two middle-aged English women driving a Morris – which the Rolls had passed earlier – stopped at the scene of the accident. 'You were going too fast,' they said, 'much too fast, but it was magnificent.'

*   *   *

Rolls-Royce doesn't indiscriminately peddle the 'best car in the world' label. Lord Hives (chairman at the time) once went on record as saying that though Rolls undoubtedly made the most expensive car in the world the Phantom II was no longer the quickest or the most comfortable vehicle on the market.

*   *   *

For many years all the road signs between Calais and Abbeville carried advertisements for Rolls-Royce.

*   *   *

The suspension of the Silver Spirit is so sensitive it even compensates for the gradual emptying of the petrol tank.

*   *   *

Scotland Yard has two bulletproof Rolls-Royces. They do not have blue lights on the top.

*   *   *

Ernest Wooler became Royce's first apprentice in 1903. In his memoirs Wooler recounts that when he was a child Royce, a family friend, had explained to him why taper bolts were preferable to rivets, the usual method of fastening metal to metal in those days. A hot rivet never fills the hole it has been put into when it cools. A cold rivet puts too much strain on the metal

91

From the outside it looks like an everyday Silver Wraith . . .
. . . But inside, the Maharanee of Baroda had some optional extras fitted, designed to take a passenger's mind off the ticking of the clock

(*facing page*) . . . And some more, designed to make sure they looked presentable when they staggered out at journey's end

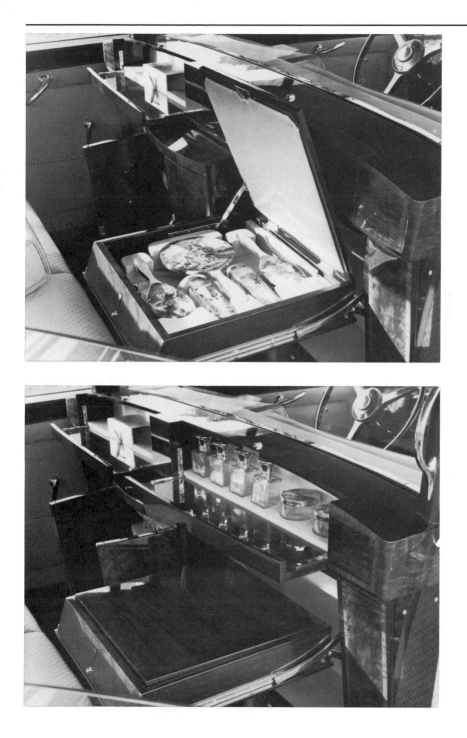

around it. So rivets never appeared on Royce or Rolls-Royce cars: taper bolts machined to fit perfectly in a hand-reamed hole were used instead.

* * *

During the First World War Rolls-Royce made rifles.

* * *

To test the durability of the seats, Rolls-Royce use 'Squirming Irma', a 200-pound simulated bottom that squirms on the seat being tested up to one million times. There is no truth in the story that this device replaced a Mrs Irma Dugdale, pensioned off in 1952 after thirty years' faithful service.

* * *

The hydraulic tappets on a Rolls-Royce engine are assembled the hard way – while immersed in paraffin to avoid the slightest contamination by dust.

* * *

Many years ago one of Britain's top silversmiths, Sidney Sparrow of William Comyn & Sons, started making two models of the 1906 Silver Ghost.

He died when the models were only partly finished and for several years they gathered dust in Comyn's workshops, no other silversmith being willing to take on the incredibly pains-taking task. Until 1981, that is, when they were finished by Geof-frey Kelsey of Comyn's in time for the Silver Ghost's 75th anniversary.

Years of research and work as well as a fair amount of solid silver went into the models. They are each valued at £100,000, nearly twice the price of a full-sized Rolls-Royce Silver Spirit.

* * *

The phrase 'the best car in the world' is usually attributed to motoring correspondent James Peacock Holland who travelled in the Silver Ghost on its famous 15,000-mile reliability run. The motoring correspondent of *The Times*, Auriga, also often quoted as originator, used the phrase some months later.

* * *

'The wonder is a Rolls-Royce exhibited by the Hon. C. S. Rolls of London. It is so silent that it has been found necessary to place a 'tell-tale' on the dashboard in order that the driver may know whether or not the motor is in operation. It sounds like a fairy tale, but it is true. To prove it, a duplicate car is kept on the street for demonstration, and in a 2-hour run with Mr Rolls the writer was unable at any time to detect the faintest sound from the motor.' (*New York Herald*, 4 December 1906.)

* * *

Two Labour politicians showing an unhealthy interest in a 1949 Bentley Mk VI coupé: Sir Stafford Cripps, Minister of Economic Affairs, and Mr J. H. Wilson, President of the Board of Trade

A modern Rolls-Royce will support the weight of a fully grown African elephant with only $1\frac{1}{2}$ inches of give. Rolls-Royce does not recommend this.

*   *   *

For many years the chromium-plated parts of Rolls-Royce cars were not electro-plated as on other cars but 'close-plated'. This means that the parts were wrapped by the tinsmith in a thin sheet of chromium plate which was then soldered in place.

*   *   *

It takes over 800 man-hours to make the body of a Phantom VI.

*   *   *

An early director of Rolls-Royce was once asked, 'How fast does your assembly line move?' 'I think I saw it move last week,' he answered.

*   *   *

A 1910 Silver Ghost was once sold to power pumps in a Welsh coal mine.

*   *   *

Until the late 1930s all Rolls-Royce cars had an exhaust-bypass switch to increase maximum speed. This made the cars so noisy that it was even then completely illegal.

*   *   *

95

At one time even the clips that held a Rolls-Royce's tools were tested to destruction. A special rig was built which repeatedly inserted and removed dummy tools thousands of times until the clips broke.

* * *

In 1910 Henry Royce built a test rig that could age a car five years in one day.

* * *

Rolls-Royce have paint-testing compounds in Crewe and Miami, Florida. Painted panels are exposed to the elements for set lengths of time and then sent back to the laboratories to see how they have weathered. It is reckoned that one year in Miami ages paint as much as five in Crewe.

* * *

Rolls-Royce may not have been the first to use the classically proportioned radiator that became their trademark. Towards the end of 1903 the Norfolk car company went out of business and many of the people they laid off came to work for Royce & Co. It is often said that these craftsmen passed on the design of the Norfolk radiator to their new employer. Undeniably, the Norfolk radiator did bear a very close resemblance to the shape Rolls-Royce made famous.

* * *

It takes one man one day to make a Rolls-Royce radiator. Five hours are then spent polishing it.

* * *

Of the twelve craftsmen who make radiators for Rolls-Royce cars, no two make them exactly the same. Each man can recognize his own work if he sees it on a car in the street.

* * *

The brass wheelnuts on a Rolls-Royce are threaded in opposite directions on opposite sides of the car so that the rotation of the wheels tends to tighten them.

* * *

You can stand a $2\frac{1}{4}$-ton Silver Spirit on four Wedgwood bone-china cups. It was done at the Wedgwood factory in 1981.

* * *

The Rolls-Royce radiator was not registered as a trademark until 1974.

* * *

Rival car manufacturers were quick to get their knock in at the new Silver Ghost and its 40/50 h.p. engine. One called it a 'triumph of workmanship over design'; another said, 'Ah yes, a wonderful car – if you can afford to use 30 horsepower to silence the 15 that do the work'.

*　　*　　*

Every crown wheel and pinion in the differential of Rolls-Royce cars are mated together by hand before being sealed in their casing to ensure absolutely silent running.

*　　*　　*

A prototype Bentley, the Corniche 4-door saloon (chassis 14BV) was being tested in France at the outbreak of the Second World War. It was dive-bombed by German Stukas – and a revolutionary new design was blown to bits. In 1945, it is said, the Rolls-Royce representative in Dieppe presented the company with all that remained of the car – the ignition key.

*　　*　　*

'Three glass tumblers were balanced upon the bonnet of a 6-cylinder 40/50 h.p. Rolls-Royce. These tumblers were then filled to overflowing with water coloured with red, green and black ink respectively. The engine was started, the starting handle removed and a revolution counter put on the end of the crankshaft. A photograph was then taken of the glasses, an exposure of exactly 4 minutes being given during which the engine revolved 4,600 times at 1,150 revolutions per minute. The experiment was repeated and notwithstanding the glasses having previously been filled to the upmost, NOT A DROP of liquid was spilled from them at any time, and the sharpness of the outlines in the photograph shows the absence of vibration in a most conclusive manner. A further test has since been made by balancing a penny on its edge on the cap of the radiator for 2 minutes, while the engine was running, thus proving that vibration is practically non-existent in a Rolls-Royce engine. To stand a penny on its edge is not an easy matter even on a rigid surface.' (From the Rolls-Royce Catalogue 1910–1911)

*　　*　　*

To demonstrate its tractability, the 1905 20 h.p. car was started in top gear with nine grown men on board on Jasper Road, Sydenham, South London, a gradient of one in six.

*　　*　　*

In 1908 a 40/50 6-cylinder Rolls-Royce Phantom would have cost you £985. That was just for the chassis. A standard body built by Barkers would have cost you £119 extra.

* * *

It takes three months to build a Silver Spirit.

* * *

The exhaust system of the Silver Spirit has six separate silencer boxes, each acoustically tuned to suppress a different range of sound frequencies.

* * *

Engineers spend up to four days 'sweetening' (i.e., removing the tiniest flaw) the bare body shell of a Rolls-Royce before the 14-stage painting process begins.

* * *

'When the engine is running one can neither hear it nor feel it.' (*The Times*, December 1904.)

* * *

You could drive a modern Rolls-Royce from the Arctic Circle to the Equator without having to adjust the air conditioning – the interior temperature would remain constant.

* * *

The number plate RR1 was sold in 1968 for more than the price of the Silver Shadow to which it was attached.

* * *

In some respects the press launch of the Camargue was not a complete success. Of the twelve cars sent down to Sicily for the press to play with seven were damaged by understandably enthusiastic journalists. In one incident the driver swerved violently to avoid an oncoming truck in a tunnel and sent £83,000 worth of car ricocheting along the tunnel walls. The shocked silence after the car came to rest was broken by the imperturbable public relations man from Rolls-Royce, Dennis Miller-Williams. 'Does anyone have a cigarette?' he asked calmly from the back seat.

* * *

About fifteen years ago a flagpole fell on the radiator of the Queen's Phantom. The radiator was dented slightly, but its soldered joints never opened. The flagpole has never been the same since.

* * *

Engineers use a stethoscope to check the smooth running of Rolls-Royce engines.

* * *

And there is a heat sensor in the Silver Spirit that automatically adjusts the temperature in the car to compensate for the heat gain from the direct rays of the sun.

* * *

The cooling capacity of the air-conditioning system in the Silver Spirit is equivalent to that of thirty domestic refrigerators.

* * *

The Rolls-Royce bible: Claude Johnson had extracts of Royce's correspondence to the Derby factory published as a guide to the engineers. Leather-bound volumes are still kept in a safe at the factory.

* * *

The Silver Ghost had 99 lubrication points, which, according to the manual, were supposed to be attended to every week. The Phantom was one of the first cars to be fitted with a centralized lubrication system whereby all important points could be lubricated from one point.

* * *

The valve seats in a modern Rolls-Royce are given a natural finish of a 16-millionth of an inch.

* * *

When, in the twenties, the quality of Continental roads began to make high-speed cruising in a car possible for the first time, Rolls-Royce issued a mild warning about running their cars at *continuous* full throttle on the *Autobahn* and *autostrada*.

Mercedes issued a similar warning that their 38/250 model should not be run at maximum output for more than 20 seconds at a time.

* * *

It has not been unknown for directors of Rolls-Royce to receive blank cheques through the post and a request for the latest model.

* * *

The finished components of early Rolls-Royce automatic gearboxes were always kept in airtight glass cabinets to protect them from the atmosphere before being assembled.

* * *

Rolls-Royce called back all the Silver Ghosts made between October 1924 and mid-1925. This was because the company had announced the introduction of four-wheel braking on all Ghosts at the 1924 London Motor Show, but various setbacks prevented the new system from going into production on time. Having announced the innovation, Rolls-Royce felt obliged to call back all cars sold after the Motor Show in order to modify them.

*   *   *

The oldest-known Rolls-Royce still on the road is the 1904 10 h.p. owned by Mr Thomas Love Jr of Scotland.

*   *   *

The Bentley Mulsanne Turbo, weighing 2 tons, accelerates from 0 to 60 m.p.h. in 7 seconds – outpacing some Ferraris. Even more astonishing for such a bulky car is its performance from 60 to 90 m.p.h. – also 7 seconds.

*   *   *

So tranquil is the interior of the Bentley Mulsanne Turbo that an eminent motoring journalist fell asleep in the rear seat while being driven at 135 m.p.h. down the Mulsanne straight at Le Mans.

*   *   *

The quality remains long after the price is forgotten.

H. Royce, Mechanic

 *The Heroes*

Show me a hero and I'll write you a tragedy.

Scott Fitzgerald

The Silver Ghost

The Heroes

Admiral Sir Miles Messervey, head of the British Secret Service, and better known to you as 'M', was chauffeured between Blades (his London Club) and his Regent's Park office at Universal Export in a black Rolls-Royce Phantom.

His most famous operative drove, to put it mildly, a Bentley. (At least he did in most of Ian Fleming's books. In the films he switched to an Aston Martin and other more exotic vehicles.) Originally it was 'one of the last of the $4\frac{1}{2}$-litre Bentleys with the supercharger by Amherst Villiers'. But after the frightful Sir Hugo Drax broke its back with a quantity of giant toilet rolls in *Moonraker*, Bond bought (in *Thunderball*) 'the most selfish car in England – a Mark II Continental Bentley that some rich idiot had married to a telegraph pole on the Great West Road'. Bond bought the bits for £1,500 and Rolls-Royce 'straightened the bend in the chassis and fitted new clockwork – the Mark IV engine with 9.5 compression'.

Rolls-Royce rewarded James Bond ill for his efforts at saving the world for capitalism as we know it. In *On Her Majesty's Secret Service* we learn that the chaps at Conduit Street had invalidated the warranty on James's car, because Bond, against all the solemn warnings of Rolls-Royce (but figuring no doubt that when you're up against heavies like Ernst Stavro Blofeld you need all the help you can get) fitted an unauthorized Arnott supercharger to the mighty engine.

This unsympathetic treatment of one of the most distinguished Owners of all is surprising, since there is a stirring heroic tradition in the story of Rolls-Royce. And some of the real-life exploits are at least as Bondian as those of 007, from those of Captain Sadlier-Jackson who in the 1914–18 War charged a troop of Uhlan cavalry in his Rolls-Royce, to that of the indefatigable Stanley Sedgwick, who in 1973 performed what has been called the longest U-turn in history, in a Corniche: Dunkirk to Marseilles *and back* between morning coffee and dinner.

Read on then, and marvel at the deeds of these dashing gentlemen – record breakers and war heroes, who (in Harold Nockold's imperishable phrase) 'made the Name the pride of Britain, the envy of the world'. And, if you find it all a bit *Boy's Own Paper*, reflect that in the early 1940s a handful of these heroes and a few hundred Rolls-Royce engines played the most deadly game in history and, fortunately for the rest of us, won.

*　　*　　*

We start, appropriately, with the first and most quintessential of all Rolls-Royce heroes – young Charlie Rolls who, in addition to his adventures in the Wright brothers biplane, was the first Englishman to break a world land-speed record.

Before he met Royce, Rolls spent much of his energy trying to capture the land-speed record from the French. In 1903, at Chipstone, Nottinghamshire, his dream came true – almost. Watched by a team of excited officials from the Automobile Club of Great Britain and Ireland he stormed round the Duke of Portland's private motor-racing course in his brand new 70 h.p. Mors Dauphine. The timekeepers clocked him at 26.4 seconds for the kilometre: 84.73 m.p.h. and over 1 m.p.h. faster than Arthur Duray's world record. To the extreme annoyance of the British, the Automobile Club de France (then the governing body for world records) refused to ratify Rolls's figures on the grounds that they didn't approve of the timing method employed.

*　　*　　*

Exactly eighty years after Charles Rolls set a new land-speed record, Richard Noble did the same. On 5 October 1983 Noble (or 'Nobbles' to his intimates) took his car, *Thrust II*, on a $5\frac{1}{2}$-second ride into immortality in Black Rock Desert, Nevada, by travelling at 314 yards a second (on the faster half of the journey) to capture the land-speed record for Britain: 633.468 m.p.h. *Thrust II* was powered by a Rolls-Royce Avon aero-engine that Noble had acquired from the Royal Air Force at a 'fairly nominal price' after it had reached its retirement age of 600 hours in a Lightning fighter. The car covered 1 mile in a fraction over $5\frac{1}{2}$ seconds – that is to say that Richard, like Superman, was travelling faster than a speeding bullet. Afterwards the new world-record holder said: 'There's going to be one hell of a party.' His wife said: 'Never again.'

*　　*　　*

Between 1905 and 1914 Rolls-Royce cars did pretty well at motor racing.

In 1905 Rolls with co-driver Massac Buist set up a world record for the drive from Monte-Carlo to Boulogne – 28 hours 14 minutes (beating the old record by 3 hours 21 minutes).

In 1906 Rolls won the Isle of Man Tourist Trophy Race by 27 minutes. In the same year Rolls won the New York 5-mile race in 5 minutes $5\frac{1}{2}$ seconds – a new record.

In 1907, Rolls, Johnson, Platford and Macready more than doubled the world record for a non-stop run (14,371 miles). In the same year a Rolls 20 h.p. model broke the world 5-mile record for 60 h.p. cars!

In 1908 a Rolls-Royce 40/50 h.p. won the Royal Automobile Club 2,000-mile International Touring Car Trial.

In 1911 E. W. Hives took a 40/50 h.p. from London to Edinburgh in top gear, beating all previous records for the run. At Christmas the same year, a stripped-down 40/50 h.p. (with Hives again at the wheel) did an amazing 101 m.p.h. at Brooklands.

In 1912 four Rolls-Royces dominated the most arduous race ever held: the Austrian Alpine Trial. (And the day *before* the race, Radley, the winning driver, won a bet of a thousand crowns (£250) that he couldn't drive 400 miles to Klagenfurt and back between sunrise and sunset.)

In 1913 a Rolls-Royce driven by Don Carlos Salamanca won the first Grand Prix ever – the Spanish Grand Prix. In November of the same year, an open-bodied Rolls-Royce broke the world record for the London–Monte-Carlo run in 26 hours 4 minutes.

*   *   *

In 1914 James Radley again won the ferociously difficult Austrian Alpine Trial. This now included a supposedly unclimbable hill – the Turracherhohe. Radley used his 'rest' day to drive 250 miles to inspect this monster, and the following day conquered it with ease.

*   *   *

One of the few early failures (in the Isle of Man Tourist Trophy Race) was marked by a famous telegram. Percy Northey, ace Rolls-Royce driver, had his car eliminated by suspension failure. His despairing telegram to Royce: 'Broken spring. Broken heart. Northey.'

*   *   *

The day after the outbreak of the First World War the War Office asked Julian Orde, secretary of the Royal Automobile Club, to provide four cars and drivers ('the last word in speed and reliability') to act as King's Messengers in France.

The next day four Rolls-Royce cars and their drivers drove into Whitehall. Forty-eight hours after the War Office's request, these motorized King's Messengers were on active service in France. Their proud boast was that their daily run between Abbeville and Boulogne was, despite heavy enemy bombardment, on a 'you can set your clocks by 'em' basis.

*   *   *

As the fighting in France grew more intense, a number of titled Owners gritted their teeth and handed over their most prized possession to the war effort. The Maharaja of Patiala gave a beautiful teak-and-aluminium-bodied Rolls-Royce to the British Expeditionary Force, to serve as a staff car for British officers. About the same time Baron Rothschild appeared at General French's HQ. He offered himself, his chauffeur and his Rolls-Royce as volunteers. At first the chauffeur did all the driving, then the gallant, but less skilful, Baron took over. At a bloody skirmish near Compiègne, the Baron swerved at a sentry's challenge and skidded into a telegraph pole. The car was temporarily crippled, the Germans were advancing; the Baron did the only thing a patriotic Owner could do. In front of an amazed troop of passing cavalry, he stripped the car of everything that could be removed, then, in a frenzy of desperation he beat the engine to scrap with a sledge-hammer. (One witty cavalry officer attached the speedometer from the Baron's car to his horse.)

*　　*　　*

During the retreat from Mons the beautiful Duchess of Cazes, determined that the family Rolls-Royce should not fall into the hands of the Germans, gave it 'for the duration' to a grateful English officer. It did 50,000 miles without a single overhaul in ghastly conditions. After the war it was returned to the Duke's *château*, still running as smoothly as ever.

*　　*　　*

The royal family's introduction to Rolls-Royce motoring was in the First World War: both King George V and the Prince of Wales, later Edward VIII, were regularly chauffeured to the front, invariably in a Rolls-Royce. This led to the Prince's becoming the first British royal Owner.

*　　*　　*

The Prince of Wales was being driven through the most dangerous part of the front, at Vermelles Ridge, during a round-the-clock bombardment by the Germans. A piece of shrapnel burst through the windscreen and killed his driver. The Prince took the dead man to a casualty clearing station, continued his tour of the front and then drove back to General Headquarters. The body of the same car was later sent to Derby and fitted to the first British royal Rolls.

*　　*　　*

In 1916 Monsieur Louis Kohn found himself trapped in a narrow road by German troops. He reversed for $4\frac{1}{2}$ kilometres ($2\frac{3}{4}$ miles) at breakneck speed under a continuous hail of bullets until the car could turn round.

*　　*　　*

Many generals, French as well as British, owned Rolls-Royce motor cars. General Foch arrived at Versailles for the signing of the peace treaty in 1919 in a Rolls-Royce. General Gourand drove his 100,000 kilometres (62,500 miles) without a service. Marshall Pétain owned one. And General French, Commander-in-Chief of the British forces, wrote a letter to Rolls-Royce in praise of his car. It was subsequently used in their publicity General Lord Kitchener ordered three Rolls-Royces. The last one – green with black edging – was completed in 1918, after Lord Kitchener had met his death at sea on a voyage to Russia. It was taken over by Lloyd George.

*   *   *

One of Kitchener's Rolls-Royces was painted bright yellow so that he could be easily recognized while travelling around London. On one occasion a traffic policeman, failing to recognize the great man, held him up for a few minutes. 'Knock the bloody fool down!' was Kitchener's instruction to his driver.

*   *   *

Field Marshal Sir Henry Wilson was driven in a Rolls-Royce at the front and at home. His eccentricity was a violent hatred of London taxis. One of his favourite occupations was driving around London looking for cabs and trying to force them on to the pavement.

*   *   *

The first British cars to land in France at the start of the First World War (and on D-Day in the Second) were Rolls-Royces.

*   *   *

Early in the First World War, a band of twenty-five motorists, mainly Rolls-Royce Owners, formed themselves into a volunteer force: the Royal Automobile Club corps, under the Duke of Westminster. They arrived in France looking for adventure – and found it.

Their number included Rolls-Royce's most famous pre-war rally driver – James Radley – who, when he wasn't taking General Snow for tours of inspection along the front, would go out on his own initiative, looking for action. Three times he found himself in no man's land, trapped between British and German machine-gun fire; and three times he escaped, crouched low over the steering wheel, while his car took on more and more the appearance of a colander.

*   *   *

The Duke of Westminster regularly drove up and down the front in his Rolls-Royce taking pot shots at the enemy. He always kept a couple of rifles and a belt of ammunition in the tonneau of his car for this purpose.

*   *   *

Major Sadlier-Jackson was loaned a beautiful Rolls-Royce, finished in natural wood by a wealthy Chilean, Raoul Edwards. In this magnificent car he acted as the 'eyes of the army' for General Allenby's Ninth Lancers. For two years he daily drove the Rolls-Royce along the front reporting on the enemy's dispositions. He and the car were continually peppered with bullets. The car saw front-line service in the Aisne hills, at Ypres and along the Menen Road. Eventually, it was returned, battered and bullet scarred, but still working perfectly, to its owner, with a letter from Sadlier-Jackson describing it as 'a very gallant car indeed'.

*   *   *

Monsieur Millerand, the French War Minister, owned three Rolls-Royces.

*   *   *

Clemenceau, the French Prime Minister, escaped death because of the speed of his Rolls-Royce and the skill of his driver. As he left his house in rue Franklin one morning an assassin opened fire. Coujat, his chauffeur, spun the car into a U-turn and drove off at speed. The boot was riddled with bullet holes – and the great man escaped unscathed.

*   *   *

Colonel Tom Bridges's epic drive to save Antwerp from the Hun has become Rolls-Royce legend. On an order from General French, Colonel Bridges (who'd just finished an all-night march with his men) leapt into a Rolls-Royce tourer at dawn on 4 October 1915 and made a desperate 400-mile drive across rutted country roads pocked with pot-holes and jammed with fleeing refugees. By late evening he was in Antwerp and by midnight he was haranguing a pyjama-clad Prince Albert and his cabinet. After an hour of heated argument from the determined colonel, the King and his ministers agreed to hold on until reinforcements arrived. Colonel Bridges's historic ride held up the German advance for five days.

*   *   *

At Gallipoli British officers reversed up to the Turkish lines in their Rolls-Royces, threw grappling hooks over the barbed wire and drove away, leaving huge gaps in the enemy defences and some pretty enraged Turks.

*   *   *

For thousands of wounded servicemen, the war provided a first and memorable ride in the world's best car. The reliability of the Rolls-Royce made it highly valued as an ambulance. Its smoothness of running meant it was reserved for the gravest cases. One such vehicle was lent to the American Ambulance Unit and in three years, often under heavy fire, it carried 5,000 wounded soldiers to safety.

*   *   *

Winston Churchill was responsible for the first armoured cars to be used in the British war effort. Normal Rolls-Royce cars were fitted with $3\frac{1}{2}$ tons of $\frac{3}{8}$-inch armour-plate and a machine-gun. They soon became one of the most feared weapons of the war. Two such cars (under the command of the Duke of Westminster) captured a German stronghold, the village of Roisel, by the simple expedient of driving into the main street of the village and opening fire on hundreds of German troops. The cars withstood an hour of concentrated enemy fire until the understandably disheartened Germans withdrew.

*   *   *

In the Near East a Rolls-Royce armoured car chased a Mercedes staff car at 60 m.p.h. across the Al Jazirah Desert. The British eventually got close enough to the Germans to try a few bursts of fire. The Mercedes's petrol tank was pierced and half-a-dozen German officers were captured.

*   *   *

The dashing Duke of Westminster, transferred from taking pot shots along the western front, turned in another terrific performance in Egypt, against Sheikh Sayed Ahmed and his army of Senussi tribesmen. The sheikh's speciality was savage raids against British troops followed by a swift retreat deep into the heart of one of the world's most inhospitable deserts, to the Siwa Oasis, much too distant for ordinary troops to penetrate. The Duke took four Rolls-Royce armoured cars (appropriately christened *Bulldog, Biter, Blast* and *Bloodhound*), drove 200 miles across the desert, blasted the sheikh and his 500 horsemen out of their stronghold and into the hills, and returned without a single loss.

*   *   *

It was Rolls-Royce v. the Senussi at Bir Hakim too – and in even more dramatic circumstances. SS *Tara* had been sunk by a German submarine in the Mediterranean. A handful of survivors reached the African coast but were captured by Senussi tribesmen and spirited away to the oasis of Bir Hakim. Once again the redoubtable Duke of Westminster's squad leapt to the rescue. Nine Rolls-Royce armoured cars tracked the Arabs to their lair, and after a fierce battle rescued the starving British sailors from their captors.

*   *   *

In West Africa, under General Botha, the Rolls-Royce speciality was surprise night raids against German cavalry. The great cars would lie quietly amid the brush until a German night patrol appeared. Then headlights would be switched on, and the Maxim guns would pour out their deadly fire. Rolls-Royce archives contain this graphic description of an officer's orders, by one of his troops: 'Now,' says the lieutenant, 'I want every man-jack of you to keep silent as the grave. No one to move until he hears my whistle. Then up headlights and open fire without further orders. If it works, there'll be no need to worry. If it doesn't, do the best you can to get out. I'll do what I can to help, but in the dark and in this perishin' country, that'll be precious little.' Generally, it worked.

*   *   *

In Russia, Commander Locker-Lampson drove a Rolls-Royce saloon (*not* an armoured car) 53,000 miles over the Caucasus Mountains, through the roughest terrain imaginable, often in temperatures of 40°C below zero and under constant enemy fire. It fell into ditches, rescued other cars in similar predicaments, became more and more riddled with bullet holes and was never serviced in three years of ferocious driving. The only parts that needed replacing at the end of its ordeal were a ballrace in one of the wheel bearings and two front springs.

*   *   *

Colonel T. E. Lawrence (Lawrence of Arabia) was the most ardent admirer of Rolls-Royce armoured cars as a fighting machine. 'Fighting de luxe' he called it, and said, 'It is almost impossible to break a Rolls-Royce.' Lawrence collected together a fleet of nine Rolls-Royce armoured cars and tenders (among them good old *Bloodhound* and *Blast*). You can read about his exploits in *The Seven Pillars of Wisdom*, but for a sample: in one day Lawrence and three Rolls-Royces destroyed two Turkish command posts, blew up a bridge, wiped out a regiment of Turkish cavalry, blew up another bridge and destroyed 600 pairs of railway lines. His driver, S. C. Rolls (no relation), wrote, 'The experience of driving a Rolls-Royce is one of continuous hustle'. Lawrence's comment: 'A Rolls in the desert is above rubies.'

*   *   *

T. E. Lawrence enters Damascus
in a Rolls-Royce

Once Lawrence got stuck in wet sand in an armoured car while fighting the Turks. He saved himself by stripping the armour plating from the beleaguered car and, thus lightened, the car was able to drive away.

*　　*　　*

Lawrence got stuck again – this time with a broken spring. He replaced it – dramatically – with three slats of wood cut to length by shots from his revolver, and stitched together with captured telegraph wire. The makeshift 'spring' held for three weeks and Lawrence made his triumphal entrance to Damascus on it.

*　　*　　*

Lawrence: 'All the Turks in Arabia could not fight a single Rolls-Royce armoured car in open country.'

*　　*　　*

Lowell Thomas asked Lawrence just after the First World War if there was anything he couldn't afford but would like to have. His reply: 'I should like to have a Rolls-Royce car with enough tyres and petrol to last me all my life.' He never got his wish.

*　　*　　*

111

Nearly three-quarters of all the aero-engines used by the British in the First World War were Rolls-Royce. The most popular, the Eagle, was adapted from the Silver Ghost automobile engine. It was the first successful V-shaped 12-cylinder aero-engine. It powered, among others, the Handley Page bomber, nicknamed the 'bloody paralyser'.

*   *   *

Royce designed his First World War aero-engines (the Eagle, the Falcon, the Hawk) so that 'they would keep going with more bits damaged than any other engine on earth'. One Eagle engine had its radiator destroyed and its oil tank badly punctured. The pilot, still under attack from the Germans, limped through the air for thirty minutes with virtually no oil, eventually crash-landing safely behind the British lines.

*   *   *

The lifting power of Rolls-Royce engine powered flying boats was enormous. In 1917, a Porte flying boat with five 350 h.p. Rolls-Royce Eagle engines took off from the sea off Felixstowe, Suffolk, with a small land plane on its back. After becoming airborne the two machines separated and landed perfectly safely.

*   *   *

One pilot of an FE2d fighter (Rolls-Royce Eagle engine) took on eighteen German planes single-handed. Having shot down two and damaged several others he ran out of ammunition. He continued the fight with his automatic pistol until the remainder were put to flight.

*   *   *

In 1919 the *Daily Mail* offered £10,000 for the first direct flight across the Atlantic.

On June 15 Captain John Alcock and Lieutenant Arthur Whitten Brown made the crossing, most of the time in dense fog and once coming out of a cloud to find themselves virtually upside down within 50 feet of the ocean. For the 1,890 miles they took 15 hours 57 minutes, beating the previous best time (by the *Mauritania*) by over three days.

*   *   *

Three views of Alcock and Brown's feat:

Alcock in a speech at the Aero Club: 'All the credit is due to the machine – and particularly to the engines: that is everything.'

The Field: 'The outstanding feature of the flight: the magnificent efficiency and reliability of the two Rolls-Royce engines on whose loyalty the whole adventure rests.'

Sir Winston Churchill: 'I do not know what we should most admire – their audacity, determination, skill, science, their Vickers Vimy aeroplane, their Rolls-Royce engines – or their good fortune.'

*   *   *

Rolls-Royce engines also powered the first flights from England to India (1918), to Australia (1920), to South Africa (1920, Brooklands to Bulawayo, Zimbabwe), and the first regular passenger service between London and Paris (1919) – the fare was 15 guineas and the flying time, 2 hours 20 minutes.

*   *   *

The South African flight (in the Vickers Vimy *Silver Queen*) was interrupted by a crash in the desert at Wadi Halfa. The aeroplane was a write-off, but the gallant airmen – Lieutenant-Colonel van Ryneveld and Flight-Lieutenant Quinton Brand – fitted the engines to another body and carried on. The same flight also concluded with a crash at Bulawayo. Once more, crew and engines were unharmed.

*   *   *

The Rolls-Royce 'R'-type engine which broke every world speed record – land, sea and air – was originally sketched out by Royce with his walking stick in the sand of West Wittering beach near his home in Sussex. It happened on a beautiful autumn day in 1928. Royce had been on a stroll with three of his colleagues, discussing Britain's need to retain air supremacy when, tired of walking, he said, 'Let's find a sheltered spot and have a talk.' From that chat and the simple sketch was born one of the most successful racing engines of all time – and the precursor of the Spitfire's Merlin engine.

*   *   *

A year later Royce was able to lie on his back in a haystack in the Hampshire countryside and watch Flight Officer Waghorn and his Rolls-Royce-powered Supermarine S6 win the Schneider Trophy for Britain in a world-record speed of 328.63 m.p.h. It is said that Royce used to deduce the speed of the aircraft from the pitch of the engine noise.

*   *   *

On the night before the race, a problem with the British entry needed an emergency piston change. A coachload of Rolls-Royce engineers down to watch the race were dragged out of a pub by the police and, sobering rapidly, worked through the small hours to complete the change. They were helped by gallons of black coffee made by Reginald Mitchell (who was later to design the Spitfire).

A few days later, the same aircraft (the Supermarine S6) flown by Squadron Leader A. H. Orlebar raised the absolute speed record to 357.7 m.p.h.

*   *   *

An eccentric and patriotic millionairess Owner allowed Rolls-Royce engines to break the world air-speed record once more.

In 1926 Fanny Lucy Radmall, daughter of a Camberwell box maker, became the richest woman in Britain when her husband, Lord Houston, died. She conceived a violent dislike for the Labour Government and particularly its leader, Ramsay Mac-Donald. (Her yacht *Liberty* displayed along its entire length a 6-foot high sign in electric lights: TO HELL WITH RAMSAY MAC-DONALD.) So when she heard that the Labour Government refused to finance the Royal Air Force's defence of the Schneider Trophy, she immediately wrote out a cheque for £100,000. (It has been suggested that in addition to her undeniable patriotism she was also motivated by a desire to avoid death duties.)

Thanks to Lady Houston's generosity Flight Lieutenant J. N. Boothman captured the trophy for keeps on 13 September 1931, and later that day Flight Lieutenant G. H. Stainforth took the world air-speed record up to 379.05 m.p.h.

*   *   *

A touching footnote to the Schneider Trophy success: after the Rolls-Royce engines had won the trophy outright for Britain, Royce and his designers were having tea on the lawn outside his house. Suddenly the great man said quietly, 'To look at us you'd never have thought we could have done it, would you?'

*   *   *

The first man to fly over 400 m.p.h. was Lieutenant G. H. Stainforth (408 m.p.h.) in a special Rolls-Royce 'sprint' engine which developed 2,530 h.p. – and led directly to the engine which powered the Spitfire, the Merlin.

*   *   *

Thirty years after Charles Rolls, Sir Malcolm Campbell attacked the land-speed record in *Bluebird* (named after the Nobel Prize-winning play by Maurice Maeterlinck, a friend of Campbell's),

Sir Malcolm Campbell with his
40/50 and 20/25 b.h.p.
Rolls-Royces

Sir Malcolm Campbell with his
2350 b.h.p. Rolls-Royce

using a 36½-litre 2,300 b.h.p. Rolls-Royce V12 'R'-type supercharged engine (as used in the Schneider Trophy air race!). On
22 February 1933 on a bumpy, treacherous, misty stretch of
sand at Daytona Beach, Florida, Sir Malcolm ripped up his tyres,
but made a world record of 272.46 m.p.h.

*   *   *

Campbell and Rolls-Royce did it again two years later in a rebuilt
Bluebird. Just feet from the ocean the car bumped and leapt over
the measured mile. ('The car was airborne most of the journey,'
said contemporary reports.) Despite wheelspin that removed the
tread from his Dunlop tyres, and a boggy patch that had *Bluebird*
going sideways, the 2,350 b.h.p. Rolls-Royce engine took
Campbell to 276.8 m.p.h. – his eighth world record.

*   *   *

The most frightening land-speed record in Rolls-Royce history
was Campbell's last – at Bonneville Salt Flats, Utah, in 1935.
A 12-mile swathe of the parched surface was scraped smooth.
A guideline of thick black oil was painted down the middle. Then

115

early one morning in September, Campbell set off. At 100 m.p.h. he changed up into second. At 200 m.p.h., into top. As he hit the measured mile the radiator inlet was closed for maximum velocity. The windscreen covered in oil; the cockpit filled with fumes; a tyre burst; Campbell lost the guideline. On his first run he finished in flames. On his second he braked too hard and ended up broadside on. But he passed the 300 m.p.h. barrier and, at the age of 50, achieved his ninth world record: 301.129 m.p.h.

*   *   *

The most prolific land-speed record breaker of them all was Captain George E. T. Eyston, OBE, MC. He graduated from driving a Silver Ghost in the early twenties to driving *Speed of the Wind* – a Rolls-Royce Kestrel aero-engined car in which he broke every world record from 1-hour to 24-hour.

*   *   *

In adapting the Kestrel engine to Eyston's car, some problems were encountered in getting the right parts for a redesign of the crank case. Eyston records that his problems were solved by a friendly Rolls-Royce foreman who told Eyston to come along to the factory late one night. The required parts were thrown over the factory wall.

*   *   *

The largest petrol-engined world-record-breaking car of all time was Eyston's gargantuan *Thunderbolt*.

So eager was Eyston to get the world land-speed record that the car was built in an astonishing six weeks. Its power came from two supercharged Rolls-Royce Schneider Trophy racing engines – with an output of 4,700 h.p. and a displacement of 73 litres.

*   *   *

At dawn on 19 November 1935 with thunderclouds threatening, Eyston's car was push-started by an ordinary family saloon car and then zoomed off to record a new land-speed record of 314.42 m.p.h.

*   *   *

Rolls-Royce engines lost and won the world land-speed record in twenty-four hours in 1938. Stirred by John Cobb's new record of 350 m.p.h. Eyston went out on the same course one day later and flashed over the measured mile in under 10.1 seconds: a new record of 357.5 m.p.h. *Thunderbolt* came to a sad end – destroyed by fire in New Zealand in 1939.

*   *   *

Sir Henry O'Neill de Hane Segrave broke the world water-speed record in *Miss England II*, with secret Rolls-Royce engines borrowed from the Air Ministry (two 1,800 h.p. supercharged 'R'-types).

They generated enough power to spin the small propeller at 13,000 r.p.m. – a speed that most marine engineers of the day didn't believe.

*   *   *

Someone compared putting the powerful Rolls-Royce engines into the Saunders-Roe hull of *Miss England II* to 'cramming a bomb into an eggshell'.

*   *   *

Unsuperstitiously Segrave attempted the record on a Friday the 13th in 1930. His first two attempts gave him the world record at 98.76 m.p.h. In his third, aimed at breaking the 100 m.p.h. barrier, he tried the engines at full throttle. *Miss England II* reached just short of 120 m.p.h., hit a submerged branch, smashed and cartwheeled. Segrave was rescued, but died of a punctured lung. His last words were: 'Did we do it?' The body of Halliwell, his Rolls-Royce mechanic, was found days later still wearing his goggles, still clutching his engineer's pencil and note pad.

*   *   *

Miss England II was salvaged from the bottom of Lake Windermere, Cumbria, and given a new propeller (*carved* not forged from high-speed steel, and so finely honed that the mechanics handling it complained of cut fingers). It went on to capture two more world speed records at the hands of Kaye Don who took it to 103.4 m.p.h. on the crocodile-infested Parana river in Argentina, and 110 m.p.h. on an Italian lake.

*   *   *

Kaye Don's crew on *Miss England II* included a dwarf called Tommy Fischer, the 'midget mechanic'. His job: to crawl into the narrow gap between hull and the Rolls-Royce engines for last minute tuning.

*   *   *

In 1932, on Loch Lomond, Rolls-Royce engines captured the water-speed record twice in one day. Kaye Don and *Miss England II* went first to 117.43 m.p.h., then to 120.5 m.p.h. Thus Don became the first man to travel at over 2 miles a minute on water.

*   *   *

Just before his death Royce refused permission for any further dangerous water-speed record attempts using Rolls-Royce engines. But in 1933, after Royce's demise, Malcolm Campbell got hold of an 'R'-type for his *Bluebird*.

He took it out on Lake Locarno (after a priest had sprinkled it with holy water, blessed and christened *Bluebird* 'Ucello Azurro'). Campbell had a different name for her: 'She's a proper sow to hold,' he said. But 'Ucello Azurro' came back to Britain with a new world record: 129.5 m.p.h.

*   *   *

Garfield Wood – who broke the world water-speed record five times for America – offered Campbell £15,000 for one of his Rolls-Royce engines. Campbell – ever the patriot – refused.

*   *   *

In 1939 with war only months away, Campbell, worried about the log-infested Scottish lochs, superstitious about Windermere, but seeking a world record 'Made in Britain', advertised in *The Times*: 'Wanted. A stretch of water about 5 miles long in a straight line, not less than 90 feet deep; must be in the British Isles. Will anyone knowing of such a lake or reservoir please tell Sir Malcolm Campbell, 169 Piccadilly, London W1.' Eventually he went out on to Lake Coniston, Cumbria. He came back, shouting, 'Bloody good show chaps!' to his mechanics, with a new world record of 141.74 m.p.h.

*   *   *

The Merlin aero-engine – which played a crucial role in the Battle of Britain – was originally developed entirely on its own resources by Rolls-Royce, without government aid. Hence its code name: PV 12 (PV = Private Venture). It was first flown on 12 April 1935 – in a biplane! (The Hawker Hart.)

*   *   *

The German World War II Messerschmitt 109 fighter and the Heinkel 113 fighter were flight tested with a Rolls-Royce engine. The Germans, forbidden by the Treaty of Versailles to build high-powered aero-engines, 'borrowed' a Rolls-Royce Kestrel engine that was being installed by them (for Rolls-Royce) in a Heinkel HE70 passenger aircraft.

*   *   *

In World War II, Spitfires, Hurricanes, Defiants, Wellingtons, Lancasters, Halifaxes, Mustangs, Mosquitoes, and Gloster Meteors all flew on Rolls-Royce engines.

(And in filming for the movie *The Battle of Britain* even the German aircraft were powered with Rolls-Royce engines.)

*   *   *

So critical to the war effort was the Merlin engine that, early in the war, Winston Churchill secretly ordered Rolls-Royce to present a complete set of drawings to the United States Government, in case Britain was overrun.

*   *   *

Early in the war, Goering asked German air ace Adolf Galland to name absolutely anything he needed that would help the *Luftwaffe* win the Battle of Britain. 'Just give me a squadron of Spitfires, Herr Reichsmarschall,' said Galland. Goering was not amused.

*   *   *

Lord Hives (managing director of Rolls-Royce during the Second World War) said of his company's part in the Battle of Britain, 'We were just the ironmongers.'

*   *   *

In the front hall of the Rolls-Royce factory at Derby is a stained-glass window featuring a young pilot, a memorial to all the pilots of the Hurricanes and Spitfires who defeated the *Luftwaffe*. The inscription reads: 'To the pilots of the Royal Air Force who, in the Battle of Britain, turned the work of our hands into the salvation of our country.'

*   *   *

Marshal of the Air Force, Lord Tedder (about the Battle of Britain): 'Three factors contributed to the British victory – the skill and bravery of the pilots, the Rolls-Royce Merlin engine, and the availability of suitable fuel.'

*   *   *

In 1940, Lord Beaverbrook arranged that Rolls-Royce Merlin engines be constructed in the USA. They were made in the Packard plant, Detroit. The Americans followed nut for nut and bolt for bolt a standard Merlin engine taken from a Royal Air Force store.

*   *   *

Henry Ford turned down the chance to make the world's greatest aero-engine because he thought Britain would lose the war.

*   *   *

When the American Mustang fighter arrived in Britain it was capable of 350 m.p.h. When fitted with a Rolls-Royce engine it improved to 450 m.p.h. – and became the best single-seater fighter in the world.

The fastest of all Second World War piston-engined fighters

119

was probably the Mustang P-51H, which managed 487 m.p.h.

* * *

Goering is said to have confessed that nothing could save Germany from defeat when he saw single-seater Mustang fighters (powered by Rolls-Royce engines) escorting Flying Fortresses to bomb Berlin.

* * *

Between 1939 and 1945, the total production of Rolls-Royce Merlin engines exceeded 150,000. The greatness of the Merlin engine lay in its capacity for improvement. In 1939 the Spitfire's top speed was 340 m.p.h. By 1944 it had reached 420 m.p.h. Its rate of climb was 20,000 feet in 10 minutes in 1939; by 1944 it could reach 38,000 feet in the same time. And when the Nazis sent over the flying bomb, the Merlin's power was increased still further so that Spitfires, Hurricanes and Mustangs could chase them, catch them and shoot them down.

* * *

The 'Wooden Wonder' – the de Havilland Mosquito, perhaps the most versatile aircraft of the Second World War – was powered by Rolls-Royce Merlin engines, and was stuck together with adhesives suggested by Donald Gomme of 'G'-Plan Furniture. It was built mainly by carpenters and joiners.

* * *

On 30 January 1943 two important speeches to the German nation were planned, one by Goering in the morning, one by Goebbels in the afternoon.

At precisely 11 a.m., as Goering was due to speak, Radio Berlin was forced off the air by a raid from Royal Air Force Mosquitoes. Not content with that, at exactly 4 p.m., just before Goebbels's speech, the 'Wooden Wonders' returned, and listeners to Radio Berlin were denied the pleasure of a harangue from the Nazi propaganda minister.

* * *

The low-level flights of the Mosquito were legendary. One Mosquito navigator (Sergeant Carreck), hopping across German rooftops, found half a Germany chimney pot in his lap – and a hole in the wooden fuselage. And Flight Lieutenant G. N. E. Yeates, of 248 Squadron, skimming across the Kattegat, carried away the spar and pennant of an enemy destroyer. On his return to base the German pennant was still fluttering from the Mosquito's nose.

* * *

The development of the Second World War Motor Torpedo Boat was achieved with Rolls-Royce Merlin engines – but so vital was Rolls-Royce to the battle in the air that the Government commanded the company to drop all marine work in favour of aircraft engines.

* * *

So that Rolls-Royce could make Meteor engines for Cromwell tanks, Lord Beaverbrook sent this telegram to the managing director of Rolls-Royce: 'The British Government has given you an open credit of one million pounds. This is a certificate of character and reputation without precedent or equal. Beaverbrook.'

* * *

The first motor car to land in Normandy in 1944 was Monty's Rolls-Royce, WMB 40. It landed on Day One of the Allied invasion.

* * *

The Rolls-Royce that General Montgomery used in the desert had the windscreen sloping away from the car – useful, because it meant the sun would not catch it and reveal his whereabouts to the *Luftwaffe*.

* * *

The first operational Allied jet fighter was the Gloster Meteor. It was powered by Rolls-Royce jet engines; and it established two world speed records: 606 m.p.h. in November 1945, and 615 m.p.h. in 1946.

* * *

The first turbo-prop airliner (1948) was the Vickers Viscount, powered by four Rolls-Royce Dart engines.

* * *

The principle of vertical take-off was demonstrated by the 'Flying Bedstead', a Rolls-Royce-designed craft, powered by two Rolls-Royce Nene engines, and first flown by Rolls-Royce test pilot, Ronnie Shepherd.

* * *

The world's first turbo-jet airliner was the de Havilland Comet. It revolutionized civil aviation, and flew on four Rolls-Royce Avon gas turbines.

* * *

For the technically minded, the following list of Rolls-Royce gas-turbine firsts may be of interest. We are indebted to Guy T. Smith for its compilation.

First turbo-jet to pass an official Type Test:
  Goblin, 1942
First turbo-prop powered flight:
  Trent/Meteor, 1945
First gas turbine in airline service:
  Dart/Viscount, 1950
First turbo-jet in airline service:
  Ghost/Comet, 1952
First man-carrying jet-lift flights:
  Nene/Flying Bedstead, 1953
First gas turbine in service in a warship:
  RM60/HMS *Grey Goose*, 1953
First multi-hole air-cooled turbine blade in service:
  Avon/Lightning, 1957
First scheduled transatlantic jet service:
  Avon/Comet, 1958
First thrust reverser in airline service:
  Avon/Comet, 1958
First silencing nozzle in airline service:
  Avon/Comet, 1958
First aero-derived gas turbine in marine service:
  Proteus/HMS *Brave Borderer*, 1958
First aero-derived gas turbine in service for electrical power generation:
  Proteus, 1959
First turbo-fan in airline service:
  Conway/Boeing 707, 1960
First air-cooled turbine blades in airline service:
  Conway/Boeing 707, 1960
First use of composite materials for major gas-turbine components:
  RB162, 1962
First gas turbine to reach 10,000 hours between overhauls:
  Conway, 1966
First operational, fixed-wing V/STOL aircraft engine:
  Pegasus Harrier, 1969
First 3-shaft turbo-fan in airline service:
  RB211/TriStar, 1972
First gas turbine in supersonic passenger service:
  Olympus 593/Concorde, 1976
First 3-shaft turbo-fan in military service:
  RB199/Tornado, 1980

THE SIX-CYLINDER
ROLLS-ROYCE

THE 40-50 H.P. SIX-CYLINDER ROLLS-ROYCE DOUBLE LANDAULET.

"The most smooth running petrol car."

—*Country Life*, December 29th, 1906.

The most luxurious and best appointed car for town or country.

SILENT, VIBRATIONLESS, WONDERFULLY FLEXIBLE, FAST HILL-CLIMBER, RELIABLE, AND ECONOMICAL.

Particulars on application.   **Trial by appointment.**

ROLLS-ROYCE, Ltd.,
14 & 15, CONDUIT STREET, LONDON, W.

AGENTS for LEICESTER, NOTTINGHAM, RUTLAND, AND DERBYSHIRE.. .. ..   The Midland Counties Motor Garage Co., Granby Street, Leicester.

AGENTS for NORTH RIDING OF YORKSHIRE AND DURHAM .. ..   The Cleveland Car Co., Cleveland Bridge Works, Darlington.

AGENTS, FRANCE .. ..   La Société Anonyme " L'Eclaire," 59, Rue la Boëtié, Paris.

AGENTS, UNITED STATES of AMERICA.. .. ..   The Rolls-Royce Import Co., Broadway, New York.

Telegrams : "Rolhead, London."   Telephones : 1497 } Gerrard.
                                                              1498 }

First commercial engine to be certified with fabricated (and fuel-efficient) wide-cord fan blades:
535E4, 1983

* * *

Post-war air-speed records were established with Rolls-Royce engines by Neville Duke (Hawker Hunter, 727 m.p.h.) by Mike Lithgow (Supermarine Swift, 737 m.p.h.) and Peter Twiss (Fairey Delta II, 1,132 m.p.h.).

* * *

The official record for a piston-engined aircraft is 499.048 m.p.h. It was established by Steve Hinton in a Mustang, powered by a 3,800 h.p. Rolls-Royce Griffon engine, at Mud Lake, Tonopah, Nevada, on 14 August 1979.

* * *

In 1957 Colonel J. Gordon Thompson and his son James borrowed two Rolls-Royce Griffon engines from the Canadian Navy, installed them in a 31-foot plywood and aluminium hydroplane, called it *Miss Supertest II*, and hired a professional speedboat driver called Arthur Ashbury to take a shot at the world propellor-driven record. During Ashbury's run an explosion blew off an airscoop, the cockpit filled with smoke and he cracked a vertebra – but his speed of 184.4 m.p.h. was the fastest ever.

* * *

In 1980 a British businessman, Sir Gordon White, set a record for travelling from London to New York. He made it in 4 hours 23 minutes and 30.5 seconds, office to office, using Concorde, two helicopters – and two Rolls-Royces.

* * *

One of the most remarkable peacetime journeys ever made in a Rolls-Royce was that undertaken by Stanley Sedgwick on Tuesday, 22 May 1973, in a Corniche borrowed from Rolls-Royce Motors. Between dawn and sunset, the heroic Sedgwick took the Corniche from Dunkirk (for morning coffee) to Marseilles (for lunch) and back to Dunkirk (for a well-deserved dinner). Total time for the 1,330-mile journey was 17 hours 22 minutes, giving an average speed of 76.57 m.p.h. Excluding stops for lunch and a 5-minute zizz on the return journey, average driving speed was 84.54 m.p.h.

Sedgwick estimates that he did over 1,000 miles at over 100 m.p.h., yet (he says) neither he nor his passenger was particularly tired at the end of this long run, something he attributes to the magnificent seats in the Corniche, the air conditioning and 'the insulation from outside noise'.

The journey did however consume 119 gallons of petrol.

Mr Sedgwick also completed 1,000 miles in one day in England in a vintage Bentley – but this took a quarter of an hour longer than his astonishing 1,300-mile journey in France.

* * *

Not as heroic as Sedgwick's journey, but much more bizarre, was the voyage described by Patrick Balfour in his book *Grand Tour*.

Balfour, on an omnibus in London's Regent Street in the 1930s, saw a sandwichboardman strolling towards Waterloo Place. The inscription on his board was peculiar:

To India
By Rolls-Royce car
for £34
Leaving October 18

and an address in Paddington.

On inquiry he found this trip was being planned by a Colonel Christmas who intended to do the journey in a car converted to run on gas produced from a charcoal burner on the running board. 'I am endeavouring to motor to India on charcoal, because if the people in India can be induced to use home-produced petrol instead of imported petrol, the country and the government will benefit. I calculate that 12 pounds of charcoal is equal in power to 1 gallon of petrol. The charcoal costs twopence and the petrol approximately two shillings and sevenpence. Thus to run my car on petrol would cost fifteen times as much as to run it on charcoal,' he told reporters at their departure.

Other replies to the advertisement included a woman who stipulated she should have breakfast in bed every morning and never rise before 10 a.m.; and a stone-deaf 80-year-old who had been bedridden for fifteen years but, as his servant said on the telephone, 'He's a great one for the newspapers and it keeps him nicely occupied answering all them advertisements in *The Times*.'

In the end the passengers were: Colonel Christmas; Miss Grimbleton, a spinster in her thirties; Mrs Mock, the frail wife of a colonial businessman; Mr Wates, a retired doctor; and Mr Quinney, a young lawyer.

All of this sounds like the plot for the beginning of an Agatha Christie novel. Unfortunately, they got only as far as Dover before deciding that the car had to be reconverted to run on petrol. But they did eventually make it to India.

* * *

There must be a score of contenders for the title of Most Fearless Hero in the Rolls-Royce saga. About the heroine, there can be no argument. Step forward, Mrs Bower Ismay. In the early 1930s Mrs Ismay took her lady's maid and her chauffeur on a 3,000-mile journey through Europe, then across the Sahara to the fabled city of Timbuktu, in her Phantom II limousine. The dauntless lady had only one fear – the dark. So she stopped off *en route* at Fortnum and Mason to buy her most important provision: twelve dozen candles.

*   *   *

Another Fortnum's customer was Simon Winchester who in 1983 drove a Silver Spirit (RRM 1) from the westernmost point of France (Pointe de Corsen) across Europe, through the Iron Curtain and deep into Soviet Russia. As can be imagined the car raised numberless Communist eyebrows. The Russian customs men took two hours X-raying every item in Winchester's luggage including the Oxford marmalade and the Gentleman's Relish in his Fortnum's hamper. The most moving reaction though was from a young Romanian girl. After a 2-mile ride in the Spirit, she burst into tears, sobbing 'It is out of a fairy story!'

*   *   *

The anti-hero of this chapter is the dashing John Dodd of Epsom, owner of the 'Beast', a car of which Rolls-Royce certainly did not approve. It was reputed to be the fastest car ever to travel on the public highway – at speeds of over 200 m.p.h. It had a bonnet 14 feet long; it was powered by a Rolls-Royce Spitfire engine and, worst of all, it had the famous Rolls-Royce radiator.

Rolls-Royce successfully instituted proceedings against this use of their symbol. During the ensuing court cases Mr Dodd contrived to break down in Fleet Street, thus ensuring maximum publicity for his astonishing car. At a subsequent hearing he rode to court on a white horse. And he produced a witness who claimed (wrongly) to be a direct descendant of Sir Henry Royce.

Although the 'Beast' is no longer on British roads (its heyday was the 1970s), Rolls-Royce executives can still hardly bring themselves to speak about it without shuddering.

This is the notorious 200 m.p.h. 'Beast'

℞ *The Silver Lady*
– and the Law

Buy old masters. They fetch a much better price than old mistresses.

Lord Beaverbrook

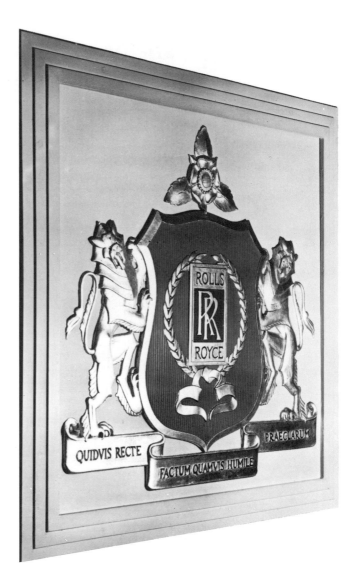

The Silver Lady
— and the Law

For the first seven years Rolls-Royce cars had no mascot at all on top of their radiator. Then, around 1910, a craze started for fitting cars with whimsical mascots. Two particularly notable examples fitted to Rolls-Royces were 'Gobbo the Lucky Imp' and a complicated device with a propeller that spun as the car moved along. Dismayed at spending several months making a car only to have it turned into an object of ridicule by an Owner with more money than aesthetic sense, Rolls Royce decided it should supply its own mascot – something suitably dignified.

Charles Sykes, a distinguished artist of the time, was introduced to Rolls-Royce by John Scott (later Lord) Montagu. Claude Johnson discussed the idea of producing a mascot with Sykes and commissioned him to come up with something. The story goes that Sykes was then taken for a ride in a Silver Ghost and, inspired by its power, silence and grace, quickly knocked out the famous statue. It has been on the radiator of Rolls-Royce cars ever since.

Along with the Rolls-Royce badge and the radiator it soon became one of the most instantly recognizable trademarks in the world. And as a result it also became one of the most widely borrowed, imitated and abused. Companies as diverse as pornographic video clubs and garden-spade makers have parodied the Silver Lady for their own ends. Sex aids have been described as the 'Rolls-Royce' of their field and stamped with the mascot. A business centre in Taiwan had plans to put up a 20-foot golden Spirit of Ecstasy on its roof and call itself the Rolls-Royce World Financial and Commercial Centre.

Fortunately there is a department at Rolls-Royce that spends most of its time persuading people against this sort of thing. In an average year it deals with about 700 cases of abuse. The Silver Lady is Rolls-Royce's greatest asset: it's surrounded by more legend and lore than any other part of the car. It is well worth protecting not just because of that, but also because without it a Rolls-Royce just wouldn't be a Rolls-Royce.

*   *   *

The model for the Silver Lady on the bonnet of every Rolls-Royce is widely believed to be Eleanor Velasco Thornton, a favourite

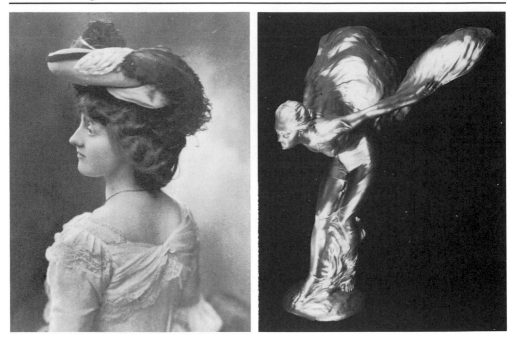

(*left*) The original model, Eleanor Thornton

(*right*) The Silver Lady

(*facing page: top to bottom*)

A selection of mascots

St George slaying the dragon: the mascot that is carried on the Queen's Rolls-Royce on ceremonial occasions

The mascot on Lord Mountbatten's car

model of the statue's creator, Charles Sykes. Her story is certainly a suitably romantic one for someone destined to be immortalized as a wind-blown sylph on the front of the most famous car in the world.

Sykes's daughter describes her in these words, 'She hated clothes, she needed to live with people who were free in their ideas. She loved life. She was an amazing woman. She definitely had quite an influence on my father's work.' Apart from being a model for Sykes, she worked for Claude Johnson (later a founder partner of Rolls-Royce) and then for Lord John Scott Montagu. She was his personal assistant and then somewhat more than that: on 5 April 1903 they had a daughter.

The end of Eleanor's story is equally dramatic. On 30 December 1915 Montague and Eleanor were sailing to Port Said on the SS *Persia* when it was torpedoed off Crete by a U-boat. They were both in the saloon when the ship was hit and, unable to reach a lifeboat, they both went down with the *Persia*, hand in hand, only to be parted by the turbulence. Montagu was fortunate enough to be wearing a quaint device known as a 'Gieve waistcoat', which was worn like an ordinary waistcoat on board ship but inflated to become more buoyant than a cork lifebelt. He rose to the surface, but Eleanor was drowned.

If Eleanor Thornton wasn't the model for the Spirit of Ecstasy, you can't help feeling that she should have been.

*   *   *

'If you ever have to open this letter it will probably be because I am no longer in the world to tell you. In the ordinary work of life I was a pioneer of motoring and she was secretary to Mr Claude Johnson. She began to like me and realized my feelings as well. Finally in 1902, in February, she became my secretary and we started *The Car*. Before long we discovered that we loved each other intensely and our mutual scruples vanished before our great love.' (Letter from John Scott Montagu to his and Eleanor Thornton's daughter. It remained sealed for thirteen years, until he died.)

*   *   *

The Spirit of Ecstasy has been somewhat irreverently called 'Miss Thornton in her flowing nightie'.

*   *   *

Jo Sykes, daughter of the original sculptor of the Spirit of Ecstasy, disputed the belief that Eleanor Thornton was the model for the mascot. She suggested that Eleanor was more statuesque than the sylph-like Spirit, but agreed that the face bears a strong resemblance to Eleanor.

*   *   *

The very first motorist to adorn his car with a mascot was, appropriately enough, the aforesaid John Scott Montagu. He mounted a model of St Christopher on his first car (not a Rolls-Royce).

*   *   *

Tom Mix earned a million dollars a year as 'King of the Cowboys'. He drove a Rolls-Royce with a silver-inlaid saddle mounted on the bonnet.

*   *   *

An agreement was drawn up between Charles Sykes, the sculptor of the original Spirit of Ecstasy, and Rolls-Royce to the effect that he was to be the sole maker and supplier of all mascots required by the company. Sykes and his small team of craftsmen supplied them for every car made up to 1948 when Rolls-Royce began producing them themselves.

*   *   *

The original 7-inch high, mascot was thought incongruous by Royce who asked Sykes to design a kneeling version. This was introduced in 1934 but was later replaced by the standing 5-inch model that still appears on the cars today.

*   *   *

The Spirit of Ecstasy on the Silver Ghost from 1911 to 1914 was the tallest of all Rolls-Royce mascots. It was also the only one finished in silver-plate, starting the kleptomania-inducing myth that Rolls-Royce mascots were made of solid silver.

*   *   *

The kneeling mascots up to 1940 are signed 'C. Sykes' with the date 26.1.34' (the date he finished the original). The earlier, standing, mascots have the inscription 'Charles Sykes, February 1911' (or sometimes 'Feb 6, 1911' or '6.2.11'). The change from full signature to initial was made for the sake of speed. All mascots up to 1951 are signed in the same way.

*   *   *

On older Rolls-Royces the Spirit of Ecstasy is often worn smooth around the waist: the result of erosion by the flapping of countless wedding ribbons in the wind.

*   *   *

In 1979, the *Daily Mirror* reported that Mr Fred Oldroyd, a meat millionaire of Bath, removed the Spirit of Ecstasy from his new Silver Shadow and had it replaced with a solid silver sausage. 'It is not the company's policy to comment on the taste of Owners,' said Rolls-Royce (which is what they said about the Beatles' psychedelic Rolls-Royce).

*   *   *

Before the design of the St George and Dragon mascot on the Queen's Phantom was finally approved it was subjected to vibration tests by Rolls-Royce engineers to check its serviceability. Structural weaknesses were found in St George's lance and the design was modified accordingly.

*   *   *

When in 1978 Jimmy Savile's new Corniche was ready for collection from Caffyn's, the Rolls-Royce dealer in Eastbourne, he walked all the way from London to collect it, crawled the last few yards and, on his hands and knees, ended by kissing the car's gold-plated mascot. Jim then took the Corniche on its first trip to present a £1,000 cheque to Variety Club of Great Britain's president, Eric Morley, at the Grosvenor House ballroom in London.

The money was raised by Jim's sponsored walk from London to Eastbourne.

*   *   *

The Spirit of Ecstasy is registered as a trademark as viewed from all angles. This closes the legal loophole which might allow someone to fit a replica of the flying lady facing sideways or backwards to a car other than a Rolls-Royce.

*   *   *

Before 1911 the Rolls-Royce had no mascot on its radiator and many Owners attached their own, including golliwogs, policemen and black cats. The Silver Lady was introduced largely to discourage this sort of thing.

*   *   *

In 1911, prior to the introduction of the Spirit of Ecstasy mascot the Rolls-Royce Board of Directors made the following statement in the *Car* and *Autocar*: 'The Directors of Rolls-Royce Limited have always taken pride in endeavouring to ensure that the outward appearance of the Rolls-Royce chassis shall be as beautiful as possible.' Purity in outline and a general appearance of elegance have in this respect been their ideals.

*   *   *

After you've bought your favourite person a Rolls-Royce why not buy a watch to go with it? Corum, the Swiss watchmakers, produce a watch in the shape of a solid-gold, diamond-encrusted Rolls-Royce radiator surmounted by a tiny Spirit of Ecstasy. These famous trademarks are used with the company's full permission, making this the only watch licensed by Rolls-Royce. It sells for around £6,000.

*   *   *

The original mascot on Bentley cars was designed by the famous motoring artist F. Gordon Crosby. Made of bronze with a massive wingspan of over 10 inches this imposing mascot was not a great success. The wings obscured the driver's view of the road and quite often fell off, damaging bonnet and windscreen. In 1932 it was replaced with the smaller winged 'B'.

*   *   *

Lord Burleigh, Marquis of Exeter and Olympic 400-yard hurdles champion, had the Spirit of Ecstasy on his Rolls-Royce replaced with the artificial hip joint that had borne his weight for ten years before being replaced. It carried the inscription: 'A loyal and faithful supporter.'

Lord Burleigh, incidentally, was the man who ran round Trinity College Great Court while the clock tolled twelve times, not, as *Chariots of Fire* has it, Harold Abrahams. He also held the record for running round the upper promenade deck of the *Queen Mary* in evening dress: 57 seconds.

*   *   *

Jackie Coogan, child star of the silent movies, had, instead of the Silver Lady, a silver and ivory model of himself in his most famous role ('The Kid' with Charlie Chaplin) perched on his Rolls-Royce.

*   *   *

The Spirit of Ecstasy mascot is produced by the Rolls-Royce Precision Components Division, the same division that produced vanes for gas-turbine engines.

*   *   *

In 1920 the Spirit of Ecstasy won a competition in Paris for the best motor-car mascot in the world.

*   *   *

Contrary to popular opinion Rolls-Royce mascots have never been made from solid silver. They have been made from various copper and zinc and nickel alloys and, in recent years, from stainless steel.

*   *   *

To trap unwary forgers, W. O. Bentley had the Bentley symbol designed with asymmetrical numbers of feathers – thirteen on the left, fourteen on the right.

*   *   *

In 1932, when Rolls-Royce took over Bentley, a competition was held to find a mascot for the new car that would bear the Bentley name. The competition was totally unsatisfactory and even the design submitted by Charles Sykes, who'd created the Rolls-Royce mascot, was rejected. It was finally decided that the 'B' for Bentley was the most acceptable and every subsequent mascot design has been based on this famous letter.

*   *   *

The 'Rolls-Royce' driven in the Paris-Dakkar rally. It is, in fact, a fibreglass imitation
Silver Shadow body on an American four-wheel drive chassis of some kind. The main
sponsor, Christian Dior, was furious when he found out

Inside the gold Rolls-Royce. All the woodwork is covered with gold leaf

Unauthorized use of
Rolls-Royce name to
imply high quality
of goods displayed

The Queen's Phantom VI is the only post-war Phantom to carry the kneeling version of the Spirit of Ecstasy. On ceremonial occasions this is replaced by the Queen's personal mascot of St George slaying the dragon, a replica of which also stood on top of her wedding cake.

*   *   *

Until recently a London firm offered a kit to convert old Austin limousines into stately Rolls-Royce cars suitable for use at weddings, funerals, receptions and so on. The kit included Rolls-Royce badges, headlights, emblems, hubcaps and even an engine plate to replace the originals. A Rolls-Royce could be hired out for about £30 an hour, but an Austin for only £15.

The deception ended after a 3-week chase around South London when the men from Rolls-Royce caught up with the managing director of and served him with a writ. Apparently he was relieved to find that his pursuers were only from Rolls-Royce and not people with designs on his well-being as well as his company.

*   *   *

On a car sent to the Maharaja of Bharatpur in the 1920s the Spirit of Ecstasy was replaced by the silver effigy of the Hindu monkey god, Hanuman.

*   *   *

Rolls-Royce does allow some use of its cars and trademarks as advertising backgrounds – if done discreetly – and licences are granted even for the manufacture of toy model Rolls-Royce cars. 'After all,' says the company solicitor, 'we would not wish to see small boys driving an inferior marque in their dreams.'

*   *   *

The Spirit of Ecstasy appears in many unlikely forms from time to time. At a dealer's reception in Exeter in 1981 a Rolls-Royce grille with mascot fashioned entirely from butter was put on display.

*   *   *

The Rolls-Royce name has even been ripped-off by pop groups: Rose-Royce the American band and the Swiss Rolls-Noise are two of the better known ones.

*   *   *

In 1947 the Rolls-Razor company sued the Rolls-Lighter company for passing off. The judge dismissed the case and said Rolls-Royce should be suing both of them.

*   *   *

The final polishing of the Spirit of Ecstasy mascot is done with powdered cherry stones.

*   *   *

The Rolls-Royce watch

The first action Rolls-Royce was ever involved in to protect any of its trademarks was against the French company Sizaire-Berwick who in 1922 started producing a car with a radiator very similar to that on a Rolls-Royce. Rolls-Royce won and Sizaire-Berwick was forced to modify the car. This episode is recounted in Jack (Dixon of Dock Green) Warner's autobiography, *Just an Ordinary Copper* – he was working as a tester for Sizaire-Berwick at the time.

*   *   *

The trademarks and name of Rolls-Royce have been misused in ways the company hardly cares to mention. A 1975 advertisement for the American men's magazine *Chic* showed a photograph of the naked backside of a woman astride the mascot on the radiator of a Silver Shadow. The headline was 'Ass with Class'.

*   *   *

The name Rolls-Royce has often been borrowed illicitly to give products or services a touch of class – as in 'the Rolls-Royce of lawnmowers' or 'the Rolls-Royce of chip shops' – but only once with Rolls-Royce's permission. Henry Royce allowed the Brough Superior motor cycle to be advertised as 'the Rolls-Royce of motor cycles' because after examining it he decided it deserved the title. The Brough Superior was, incidentally, the motor cycle ridden by that great Rolls-Royce devotee, T. E. Lawrence. (See *Heroes.*)

*   *   *

Cal Vista Video – simply not on

A distributor of pornographic videos in Los Angeles, California, Cal Vista Video, had been sending out cassettes in holders shaped like the Rolls-Royce radiator until the company stopped him. His goods were, of course, described as 'the Rolls-Royce of the adult motion picture and video industry'.

*　　*　　*

The laws of many countries now insist that ornaments projecting more than 10 millimetres (0.3 inches) above the bodywork must retract, snap or bend if subjected to a force of 22 pounds or more.

Modifying the mascot's base so that it would break under

The Rolls-Royce supermarket. One of the company's lesser-known sidelines

stress was obviously unacceptable since it could then be easily snapped off by a thief. Instead, it is mounted on a spring-loaded mechanism and retracts quickly into the radiator shell if struck from any direction. In tests, the mascot was knocked down 100,000 times by a 15-pound rubber-coated wooden ball to check the reliability of the mechanism.

*   *   *

Woodrow Wilson had a statue of the Princeton tiger on the radiator of his Rolls-Royce.

*   *   *

The Duke of Gloucester had his personal mascot, a silver model of a swooping bird, replace the Spirit of Ecstasy on his Rolls-Royce.

*   *   *

In January 1984 Mr W. E. N. Lung-Chen of 11 S. Alley, 351 Lane, Third Floor, South Road, Taipei, Taiwan, registered the trademark RR and then deliberately misspelt the name: Rolls-Rocye. He has nothing to do with Rolls-Royce, of course, but is one of the many Taiwanese who have taken advantage of their law's relaxed attitude on the subject of trademarks and commandeered a long list of names, including Raleigh, Levi Jeans, Ferodo brake linings, Sheffield Steel, Johnnie Walker, Brylcreem, Gordon's Gin, Parker pens, Dimple Haig, EMI Records and Shetland pullovers.

Somehow it seems likely that. should he ever start making cars, Mr Lung-Chen's Rolls-Rocyes will be fairly easy to distinguish from the real thing, though it might be worth checking the badge on the radiator before you part with your cash.

*   *   *

In 1978 a bronze casting of Charles Sykes's Spirit of Ecstasy was put up for sale at Christie's in New York. The sculpture, standing $30\frac{1}{2}$ inches high, went to a private buyer for $6,500.

*   *   *

Lloyd George had a winged flying artillery shell on the radiator of his Rolls, a car he inherited from Lord Kitchener.

*   *   *

Every mascot is made by the ancient 'lost wax' casting method: a wax model is made by pouring molten wax into a 'jelly mould' of the original sculpture. This wax model is then finished by hand – this is why no two mascots are exactly the same – and then set in a plaster cast. Molten metal is then poured into the cast, flowing into space left by the wax as it melts out. Bronze figures found in 4,000-year-old Chinese tombs were made by the same method.

*   *   *

From 1911 to 1928 every mascot produced was checked personally by Charles Sykes. Any that did not meet his specification in detail and finish to the face, hands and drapery were rejected.

*   *   *

So precious to Rolls-Royce is the name, the radiator and the symbol, that rarely a day goes by without the company being involved in legal action concerning their unauthorized use.

'You have to police your trademark or you lose it. We've spent eighty years building up our trademarks, and you can't expect us to let some entrepreneur climb on our back and start making money in eighty minutes.' (Lewis Gaze, Rolls-Royce company solicitor)

*   *   *

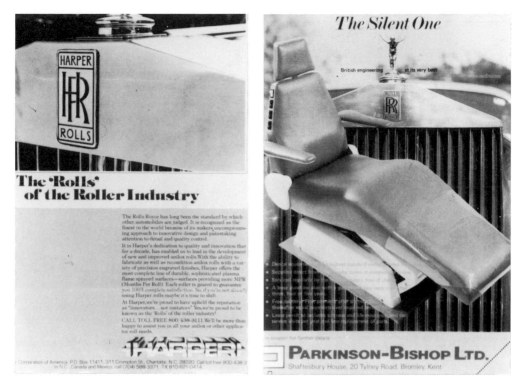
This is not allowed, either   . . . Nor this

RR-VW

The advertisement reads:

Now, the pride of Sheffield at prices to see you proud.

Now from Sheffield, the ho[me of] steel, a new range of garden too[ls to] see you proud at home.

A perfect embodiment of 2[00] years of know-how, Sheffield [makes] precision-made garden tools [for] everything for the serious gard[ener] who is equally serious about hi[s] bank balance.

We can show you the very b[est] spades, forks, trowels, shears, h[oes] and edging knives in stainless [steel,] the quality of which can only [be] matched by the sheer value — [and] quality of our Thrifty range.

Why not call in on your lo[cal] stockist and see why we take s[uch] pride in our craftsmanship — a[nd] why we're proud to be British.

SHEFFIEL[D]
Pride

The best of British to[ols]

. . . Nor this

Rolls-Royce will always be British. Should the firm fall into foreign hands, the name will die.

*   *   *

The name Rolls-Royce still belongs to Rolls-Royce Limited, the
aero-engine company, and Rolls-Royce Motors have exclusive
licence to use the name and badge on motor cars – even the
aero-engine company cannot call a motor car by that name.
Rolls-Royce Motors owns the trademarks in the radiator grille,
the flying lady mascot, all the product names and all the Bentley
trademarks.

*   *   *

 *Apocrypha*

Let us cling to our legends – they are the spiritual side of facts.
Harley Granville-Barker

The original Silver Ghost with distinguished passengers

Apocrypha

Like any other great religion, the Rolls-Royce has accumulated its share of myths:

Rolls-Royce engines are tested by balancing a coin of the realm on edge on the cylinder head at full throttle.

The Silver Lady really is made of silver.

Owners sign a declaration saying they'll never open the bonnet in public (or the warranty is annulled).

Rolls-Royce refused to sell the Silver Spirit to a well-known megastar because her behaviour was inconsistent with the traditions of the marque.

On the infinitely rare occasions when a car 'fails to proceed' (Rolls-Royce terminology), a plain black van appears after midnight and spirits the stricken vehicle away in secrecy.

Rolls-Royce does not of course encourage the spread of such fairy tales – but neither does it rush to deny them; for part of what it's selling is legend. Some of the stories are based on fact. (The coins-on-the-edge trick, for instance, was first carried out in 1910, but it's certainly not part of official procedure.) Others are pure fabrication – but their currency is an indication of the fascination the best car in the world exercises over practically all of us.

Collected here are some of the better bits of folklore. They are almost as surprising as the truth.

*   *   *

The classic, and most often repeated, piece of Rolls-Royce apocrypha dates from the 1930s but is born anew with each model. An Owner is driving a Silver Wraith (or Shadow or Corniche) in the South of France and, incredibly, his rear axle (or crank shaft) breaks. After a phone call to the nearest distributor, two men fly in from Derby (or Crewe) and in less than twenty-four hours the offending part is replaced and the astonished Owner is on his way. He is even more astonished not to receive a bill from Rolls-Royce. Being (like all Owners) an honest man, he writes asking for one. The reply: 'We have no record of the incident you refer to. Rolls-Royce axles do not break.'

Although a fable, this story may have its roots in truth. In 1932 Rudyard Kipling was motoring in his Phantom in the South of France when for some reason it failed to proceed. A midnight phone call was made to the nearest distributor. Next morning Kipling chafed in his hotel waiting for someone to mend his car. At noon, he asked the hotel manager to get him Rolls-Royce, Paris, so he could complain. 'But, *monsieur*,' said the manager, 'the gentlemen from Rolls-Royce came last night.' The Rolls-Royce mechanics had driven a hundred miles in the small hours, cured Kipling's car of what ailed it, and disappeared without disturbing the Owner.

* * *

One of the first men to have a phone in his Rolls-Royce was show-biz king Jack Hylton. Shortly after (or so the story goes) Lew Grade, anxious not to be left behind in the status race, also had one installed. Naturally, his first call was to the car of his arch-rival. The devastating reply from Hylton's chauffeur: 'I'm sorry, Mr Hylton is on the other phone.'

* * *

Aristotle Onassis and Stavros Niarchos have lunch together in New York. Afterwards they pass a Rolls-Royce showroom and buy a Corniche apiece. Niarchos makes to pick up the bill. 'No, no, no, Stavros,' says Onassis. 'Let me get these – you paid for the lunch.'

* * *

It may or may not be apocryphal – Rolls-Royce won't confirm or deny it. There's a horror story in the factory about the apprentice who drove a Silver Shadow off a ramp – on to four Camargues.

* * *

And equally unconfirmed is the fabulous story of Rolls-Royce's chief demonstrator, now retired, who, in a colourful career, crashed forty-seven Rolls-Royces (three into other Rolls-Royces). If true, this is certainly a world record.

* * *

Another report we can't pin down is of the very royal Rolls-Royce that went in for a service in the 1950s, the glove compartment of which was found to be stuffed with ten-shilling notes (ladies-in-waiting, tipping, for the use of).

* * *

This story is courtesy of Oliver, the Mayfair top people's hairdresser. In the early 1970s, Mr Harry Freidenhausen, a sugar millionaire from New York, gave his wife Marion a most pleasing birthday present: a mini-sized Rolls-Royce. Rolls-Royce executives at Crewe do not have a record of this car.

* * *

Lord Denning: Master of the Rolls?

Possibly exaggerated is the one about the chap in the East African Rally who hurled his Bentley Mulsanne round a U-bend, into a ravine and on top of a Volvo which had preceded him minutes before. 'Awfully sorry, old man!' shouts the chap in the Bentley, 'Not to worry, mate. There's a Citroën under me!' replies the bloke in the Volvo.

This story does have an echo in fact. David Burgess-Wise in *Automobile Archaeology* tells of a visit to a breaker's yard in Kent in the late 1950s, where he discovered four rusting Silver Ghosts standing one on the other.

*   *   *

After Rolls and Royce got together, there arose the problem of what to call the car. Rolls said: 'I know! Let's give it our two names.' Royce was delighted: 'I like that. Royce-Rolls! Yes, it has a ring to it.'

We prefer to believe this one. Anyway, the BBC featured it in the TV drama series *The Edwardians* – so it must be true.

*   *   *

Certainly untrue is the fable that Lenin pinched his Rolls-Royce off the Tsar. As we have seen (in 'Owners'), he had Comrade Krassin buy them at the 1920 London Motor Show. The Tsar's Rolls-Royces were brought back to England by Lord Furness before the Revolution.

*   *   *

This one is true. David Roscoe, doyen of Rolls-Royce raconteurs (book him next time you want an after-dinner speaker), tells the story of the London businessman who arranged an idyllic weekend with a young lady he ought not to have been with, touring the West Country in his Rolls-Royce. Early in their tour they had to cross the River Dart by ferry. Unfortunately someone had neglected to close the front gate of the ferry. Slowly, unstoppably and to everyone's horror, the great car rolled off the ferry and into the River Dart, whence it floated downstream. Some miles further on it fetched up in Dartmouth harbour, bobbing about among the fishing boats. As David put it: 'Not only did this invalidate the warranty, it also made the ink run.' What qualifies this true story to appear under *Apocrypha* is that in some versions, the hapless couple are inside the car as it makes its epic voyage downstream.

*   *   *

That most eminent pillar of the British justiciary, Lord Denning – who ought to speak the truth if any man should – tells in after-dinner speeches that after he was gazetted as Master of the Rolls, a lady wrote to him to arrange a service for her Corniche.

*   *   *

In 1984 the Italian magazine *La Domenica del Corriere* featured an Amazonian chimpanzee that had been imported to Los Angeles and trained to wash and polish his owner's Rolls-Royce.

*   *   *

In the first days of the Second World War a lady Owner in Guernsey, fearful that the Germans would invade and misappropriate her Rolls-Royce Twenty, phoned Conduit Street for help. Within twenty-four hours two chaps in brown bowlers appeared. disassembled the Twenty and concealed it in bits in a barn. They left after reassuring the lady that, like General MacArthur, they would return. The Nazis invaded. The car stayed safe in its hiding place. Four years later when the first British landing craft beached near St Peter Port, out streamed 200 infantrymen – and two chaps in brown bowlers.

*   *   *

A Rolls-Royce Corniche Owner drives up to a petrol station in the Midwest and says to the admiring attendant, 'Fill 'er up.' The attendant starts to comply. Two minutes later he's back at the front of the car: 'Better switch the engine off, bud. She's gaining on us.'

*　　*　　*

There are numberless stories of the inconsequential way in which people choose their car. An American picked a Bentley because it was the only car that would accommodate his fishing rods. And often quoted is the story of the titled lady who sent her chauffeur out to buy the latest model. He comes back with a Bentley instead of a Silver Spirit. 'I told you to get the one with the *square* radiator!' she storms.

*　　*　　*

In 1967, at the height of the great Rolls-Royce mascot crime wave, when no Spirit of Ecstasy was safe, one unfortunate Mayfair Owner had three nicked off his Silver Wraith within a month. The final outrage came when he had to report a fourth robbery: the witty thieves had purloined the Silver Wraith and left behind the latest mascot.

*　　*　　*

According to Graeme Godfrey (whom we don't believe for a minute), in 1923 the illusionist, the Great Francetti, purchased two Rolls-Royce Phantoms. They were identical in every way except that one was 11 inches larger than the other in every dimension and it was possible, through a special system of hatches, to drive the smaller vehicle into the larger, disappearing from view.

*　　*　　*

A golden oldie: an Owner drives into a village at noon, decides to have lunch. He leaves the car for a wash and brush up at the local garage, for it has been a dusty drive.

In the process of valeting, the petrol-pump attendant comes across a pair of golf tees which puzzle him, as he had never seen such things before. When the Owner returns he is asked what the tees are for. 'For resting my balls on prior to driving off,' he replies. 'My! These Rolls-Royce people think of everything.'

*　　*　　*

The best joke involving a Rolls-Royce is the famous 'Blimey, what a driver!' story, originally told of the Rolls-Royce Corniche. It is too unsavoury to sully these pages – but if you haven't heard it, ask around any saloon bar.

*　　*　　*

149

Prakesh Patel

Classified advertisement in the *Coventry Evening Telegraph*: 'For sale: Rolls-Royce hearse with 1965 body' (quoted on the Esther Rantzen TV show *That's Life*).

*   *   *

Among the appointments carried in the rear of the Maharaja of Nohrapur's Phantom V is a cocktail shaker. His name is Patel.

*   *   *

Ian Hallows, editor of *The 20 Ghost Club Record* (of a trip in a Silver Shadow): 'Your editor noticed the loudest sound that could be heard was the beating of his bank manager's heart.'

*   *   *

In the early days of self-starters a Rolls-Royce distributor was proudly demonstrating his latest model to a customer when he was stopped cold by the query, 'Why does it carry a starting handle then?' 'Well, sir, in the extremely unlikely eventuality of the car failing to. . . .' 'Ah, you admit it then! The self-starting mechanism isn't foolproof, else you wouldn't carry a starting handle.' 'Sir,' replied the Rolls-Royce man icily, 'you know those two small bumps on your chest?' 'Yes?' 'Well, sir, if you were to give birth, they would permit you to give the infant milk. The contingency of your needing to employ the starting handle on a Rolls-Royce is about equally remote.'

*   *   *

This actually happened. At the height of the petrol crisis, when Arabs generally were coming in for a fair bit of unfavourable publicity, there appeared on the front pages of the popular British press a picture of four gentlemen from Saudi pushing a Phantom VI. The story was that, on the way from London's Heathrow Airport, their Rolls-Royce had run out of petrol, giving Fleet Street a gem of a picture. What merits its inclusion under 'Apocrypha' is that the whole thing was an April Fool's Day gag, perpetrated by a bunch of entirely British jokesters.

*   *   *

On the last day of March 1983 (i.e., the day before April Fool's Day) Rolls-Royce ran a spoof advertisement in *The Times*, containing a large number of factoids. It speaks volumes for the reputation of the car that, subsequently, hundreds of amused readers wrote to Rolls-Royce claiming to have believed every word of it until they read the obviously incredible twenty-ninth fact. We reproduce them all here.

Dieu se sert icy de moi
Pour t'anoncer de l'Angleterre,
Et portant le nom de Rolles de Roi
Une carosse silencieux, construy en fer.

Nostradamus'
remarkable prediction

Sir Arnold Windrush, Tory Member of Parliament for Fen End, had the ignominy of hearing his maiden speech in the House of Commons described by Aneurin Bevan as: 'The Rolls-Royce of speeches – it was smooth, inaudible and seemed to go on for ever.'

*　　*　　*

151

Henry Royce's real name was Henry Runnicles. The company was called Rolls-Runnicles for the first three months of its life until, after constant pressure from Charles Rolls, Runnicles changed his name to the more euphonious Royce.

*   *   *

Having lost his considerable fortune gambling, Viscount Arthur 'Dodgy' Rumplemere was arrested for drunkenness in 1923. Appearing in court, he gave his address as a Rolls-Royce Silver Ghost parked on the Thames Embankment. After serving a ten-day prison sentence he returned to his residence and continued to live there until he died in 1952. The car was started without difficulty for the first time in twenty-nine years, to carry Viscount Arthur to his last resting place.

*   *   *

Incredibly, Nostradamus in 1548 made this prediction: 'From Albion's shore shall come a marvellous contryvance: a carriage silencieux bearing the arms of Rolles de Roi.'

*   *   *

Until 1933 no Rolls-Royce was equipped with a reverse gear. Sir Henry Royce was unwilling to have his car adopt what he regarded as an undignified mode of progression.

Every Spirit of Ecstasy mascot, after its final polishing, is wrapped in moistened tobacco leaves and stored in the dark for twenty-one days. This practice was first adopted in 1911. No one working for the company now remembers why.

*   *   *

On the exceedingly rare occasions when an Owner is moved to raise the bonnet of any post-war Rolls-Royce, he hears a discreetly modulated rendering of 'Land of Hope and Glory' played by the BBC Symphony Orchestra.

*   *   *

Examine closely the number plates on the Silver Spirit. Each one is hand-painted by a student from the Crewe College of Art.

*   *   *

In 1934 the far-sighted Mayor of Blackpool, Alderman Billy 'Progress' Bickerstaffe, decided to replace the entire Blackpool tram fleet with Rolls-Royce motor cars. Sadly, the company was not prepared to modify the car for overhead cables.

*   *   *

Not everyone prefers the modern Rolls-Royce: Monsieur Raoul Bergerac (37) of Clermont-Ferrand (the human waste-disposal unit), who is currently trying to eat an entire 1983 Silver Spirit, told reporters: 'Ça va, mais ça manque le goût delicat de l'ancien Phantom V.' (Nice, but it doesn't have the exquisite flavour of the old Phantom V.)

*   *   *

Shostakovich's opus 86, *The Rolls-Royce Symphony* dedicated to Stalin's favourite mode of travel, was renamed in 1959 (during the era of de-Stalinization): 'Hymn to the glorious achievements of Soviet workers in the coal, petroleum derivatives and animal foodstuff sectors of production'.

*   *   *

Just after the Second World War Rolls-Royce diversified into adult tricycles. Some 200 of the 'best tricycles in the world' were produced before the venture was deemed unprofitable. Needless to say these vehicles are now collector's items.

*   *   *

In 1939, Adolf Hitler's attempt to buy the only Silver Wraith in the Third Reich was frustrated by a midnight phone call from Rolls-Royce's Conduit Street office, ordering the car into Poland. After a 300-mile drive the car crossed the border pursued by an entire Panzer division. The date was 1 September. The rest is history.

*   *   *

Extras fitted to Rolls-Royce cars have included a spiral staircase, an interior depicting the Battle of Lepanto, an integral Black and Decker Workmate, a nuclear fall-out shelter, and a one-twentieth scale model of the Leicester Square Odeon.

*   *   *

The air conditioning on the Silver Spirit is so refined that Owners have the choice of ten atmospheres, ranging from dawn at Simla to late evening on the Promenade des Anglais to Sunday morning on the sea front at Bournemouth.

*   *   *

The Rolls-Royce radiator was long thought to have slightly curved rather than straight sides to give the illusion of rectilinearity, like the Parthenon. Not so. It is thus because the ruler of Arthur Throat, the man who crafted the very first radiator, was warped.

*   *   *

In the province of M'bnga, in Lower Volta, a Rolls-Royce is worshipped as the supreme deity. It was brought to the area in 1911 by the missionary Sir Archibald Cameron, whose rudimentary knowledge of the M'bnga dialect led to some confusion between the appellations 'Silver' and 'Holy' Ghost. Sir Archibald was eaten before he could correct the unfortunate misunderstanding.

*   *   *

When a man becomes a Rolls-Royce chauffeur, he must choose a new surname to be used in the course of his work. He has to make his choice from the names of the original team of Rolls-Royce chauffeurs: Cartwright, Crawford, Felpin, Oakes, Swadling, Tidmarsh, Wiggins and Xianapopoulos.

*   *   *

In the late 1930s Rolls-Royce and the police of five continents were baffled by the sudden appearance of some very bad copies of the Rolls-Royce Phantom. They were finally tracked down to a small workshop in County Tyrone owned by a Mr Patrick O'Reilly. The car (the 'Rolls O'Reilly') had an unusually loud engine and an even louder clock. Hence the advertising slogan, 'At 60 m.p.h. the loudest noise in the Rolls O'Reilly is the tick of the clock.'

*   *   *

Underneath the hallowed turf at Crewe Alexandra Football Club is buried an entire Rolls-Royce.

*   *   *

NASA's latest Voyager space probe contains a time capsule in the form of a complete Rolls-Royce Silver Spirit.

Earth's most famous car is at the moment passing Jupiter and is expected to reach the outer planets around the year 1990. It contains copies of the Bible, the Complete Works of Shakespeare, and *Jonathan Livingston Seagull*, together with an LP record (*Kiri te Kanawa Live at Wembley Stadium*) and a video recording of the *Coronation Street* episodes documenting Ken's and Deirdre's marital crisis.

*   *   *

The wheels on the 1983 Silver Spirit are based on a 6,000-year-old design principle first established by the Sumerians.

*   *   *

In 1915 Major D'Avigdor-Simpson, DSO, drove his Silver Ghost 23,000 miles across the Siberian wastes at temperatures as low as 50° F below zero. After three months of such driving he and

Rolls looks dismayed as the brakes fail on a early experimental car and he careers towards a group of weekend guests playing croquet on the lawn of his father's house

his car skidded into the icebound River Yenesei, whence they floated into the Arctic Ocean. Three years later the car, frozen solid into the pack ice, was picked up by a Russian cargo ship. On reaching Murmansk, the vehicle and its driver were thawed out. The Silver Ghost started first time – which is more than can be said for the gallant major.

*   *   *

There are no Rolls-Royce motors cars in Ulan Bator.

*   *   *

It takes one craftsman one week to produce a Rolls-Royce radiator. All the other craftsmen manage one a day.

*   *   *

Henry Royce once came upon a young mechanic using a steel rule to check the dimensions of a radiator he'd just completed. Incensed at this use of artificial aids, Royce battered the misguided youth to death with the implement. To this day, the company still pays a pension to his family.

*   *   *

Twenty years after buying his Phantom in 1929, the Maharaja of Nohrapur sent a small urn to Rolls-Royce at Crewe containing the mortal remains of one Wilfred Crampton, a Rolls-Royce tester.

Apparently Wilfred had heard the suspicion of a rattle just before the car left the company. He climbed into the boot to investigate and was accidentally locked in.

Not wishing to give the new owner any reason to be dis-

155

satisfied he had quietly expired there. In explanation of the delay, the Maharaja said he had had little recourse to the boot.

* * *

Mr Neil Anderson of Welwyn, Hertfordshire, is the Owner of the only wind-driven Rolls-Royce – a special adaptation designed by himself.

* * *

While test-driving a prototype of the new Bentley Turbo on a disused airstrip, two Rolls-Royce engineers noticed a Cessna aircraft attempting an emergency landing behind them. The only alternative to a disastrous collision was to use the power of the Turbo, as yet untested to its fullest potential, and accelerate out of danger.

To the astonishment of the engineers, the car cleared the perimeter fencing by 6 inches and continued to rise to a cruising height of 1,500 feet.

* * *

The rear arm rests in the Silver Spirit are edible.

* * *

In 1967, Miss Gladys Moncrieff, after a heavy dinner at the Shelbourne Hotel, Dublin, fell asleep at the wheel of her 1924 Silver Ghost on the drive home. The magnificent old car completed the remaining 23 miles of the familiar journey unassisted, and on arrival at the family residence summoned Miss Moncrieff's sister Amelia with a series of gentle toots on the horn.

* * *

Each word in every Rolls-Royce advertisement is checked by a committee of four: the Editors of *The Times* and of the *Oxford English Dictionary*, a lineal descendant of Peter Mark Roget, and the Archbishop of Canterbury.

The process takes about four months.

* * *

In 1911 the normally humourless Henry Royce played an April Fool's Day joke on his employees: he presented them all with exploding cigars. The date of his prank (due to Royce's failure to purchase a new calendar) was in fact 31 March – but none of his staff dared to point this out.

Subsequently, the incident gave rise to the tradition, which continues to this day, of premature April Fool's jokes at the Rolls-Royce factory.

* * *

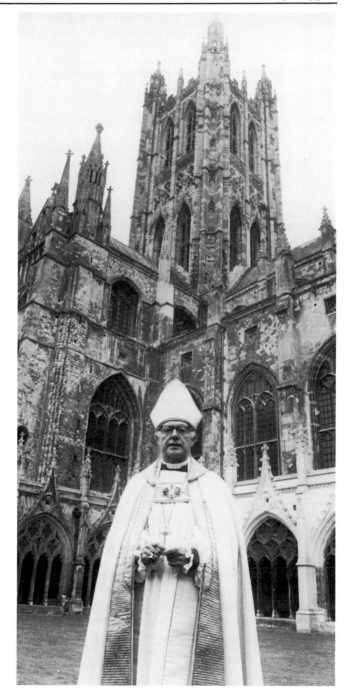

The Archbishop of Canterbury,
without whom this book would
not have been possible

One of the best apocryphal Rolls-Royce tales was told by Art Buchwald, twenty years or more ago, in the *New York Herald Tribune*. It was then reprinted in his book *More Caviare*. We are indebted to Mr Buchwald for permission to reproduce it here.

It's a Rolls-Royce Period

Art Buchwald

Many people, mostly friends, have accused me of being in the employ of the Chrysler Company because I used an Imperial on my trip to Russia. The least they thought I'd get out of the trip was a car. I must categorically deny the accusations. As a matter of fact, at the very time the series was printed, the executives of Chrysler voted to take a cut in salary. Whether this had anything to do with the series or not I'll never know, but it certainly proves they're in no mood to give away any automobiles to journalists who drive to Moscow.

To show I have an open mind on the subject I would like to discuss now the Rolls-Royce. Hollywood is now going into its Rolls-Royce period. Director Billy Wilder, musical writers Alan Lerner and Fritz Loewe, actors Rex Harrison, Cary Grant, Bill Holden and Gary Cooper, actress Deborah Kerr and producer Sam Spiegel are only a few of the people who have bought Rolls. In Paris there is a whole school of painters, starting with Bernard Buffet and Georges Mathieu, who own Rolls-Royces, and it is said by some of their critics that they paint from their cars instead of using an easel.

In any case, there is a case for the Rolls-Royce as a means of giving someone social status.

I didn't realize the lengths to which the Rolls-Royce Company goes to keep up the reputation until I got into conversation with a Rolls-Royce chauffeur in front of the Hotel George V.

The Rolls people train their own chauffeurs. It takes four years to get a certificate, and only after he has a diploma is a chauffeur allowed to open the bonnet of the car.

There is a certain form a Rolls chauffeur must follow. 'We never brag,' he told me without bragging. 'We never attempt to say it's better than any other car.'

'What do you say?'

'We say, "It's a nice car." '

'How fast does it go?'

'We're not allowed to tell. Also, we can't mention any acceleration figures. All I can say is: "She's fairly fast." '

Among the other things I discovered is: 'One never cleans a Rolls-Royce on the street. But a Rolls must always be clean inside and out. Ashtrays are emptied daily and there must always be enough petrol so one does not have to stop at a station when the Owner is in the car.'

'Are the other chauffeurs envious when you drive up in a Rolls?'

'One likes to be modest about that sort of thing, but I'll have to admit there is a certain amount of envy. I've seen chauffeurs of Cadillac Eldorados who have had the admiration of the whole block to themselves become very annoyed when I drive up in my Silver Cloud. It's that unfortunate something the Rolls has.'

If a Rolls-Royce owner uses a Rolls-Royce-trained chauffeur, the car is guaranteed for twenty-one years. If he doesn't use a Rolls-Royce chauffeur, it's only guaranteed for three years.

A Rolls-Royce is never towed through the streets. In case something happens, a covered van is sent for and the car is placed in the van and quietly taken away.

'The bonnet of a Rolls may never be opened on the street because people might think something has gone wrong,' the chauffeur told me. 'If I opened this bonnet in front of the hotel, it would take less than two hours for word to filter into our Rolls-Royce dealer in Paris, and there would be an inspector over from London in no time.'

The Rolls-Royce radiator cap has only been changed three times. The first Spirit of Ecstasy was a nude woman standing erect, her lithe body defying the wind. The second Spirit of Ecstasy was clothed and on one knee. The present one is still clothed, but she is bent over as if she's about to do a jack-knife dive off the radiator.

You can lose your guaranty if you change the radiator cap on your Rolls to a non-Spirit of Ecstasy figure.

One of the Gulbenkians not only changed the radiator cap on his Rolls-Royce, but the radiator. The Rolls-Royce people were so hurt they took away his guaranty and his chauffeur, and vowed they would never sell him another Rolls again. He was, so to speak, drum-Rolled out of the regiment.

I noticed that the particular Rolls my chauffeur was driving did not have automatic windows, and I commented on this.

'We'll put them in if anyone insists,' he said, 'but we don't like to.'

'Why not?'

'Something might go wrong with them before the twenty-one years is up.'

I was embarrassed, but I couldn't control myself any longer, and I finally said: 'Could I have a peek at the motor?'

The chauffeur looked as if I had asked him if he beat his wife. 'I told you I couldn't open the bonnet on a public street.'

'Couldn't we go into the Bois de Boulogne where no one would see us?'

159

The chauffeur looked at his watch. 'I've got twenty minutes. Come on, let's go.'

He drove me out to a secluded spot in the Bois. I played lookout while he opened the bonnet. Then he played lookout while I looked at the motor. It was a moment I'll never forget.

I just got the bonnet back in time as two children came cycling through the woods. Many people have asked me if a Rolls-Royce motor is as good in real life as it is on the screen. And my answer to that is: 'She's better, man, better.'

(Reproduced by permission of the author)

Rolls and Royce and the Hyphen

And that's how it all began, my dears,
And that's how it all began!

Rudyard Kipling

The Hon. Charles Stewart Rolls

Rolls and Royce and the Hyphen

What would have happened if Charles Rolls and Henry Royce had never crossed paths? Would the Rolls-Runnicles or the MacSweeney-Royce now be the most famous car in the world? Or would the names of both men have disappeared completely, like dozens of others from the early days of the British car industry?

Interesting, but pointless to speculate, because the fact is that, by one of history's happier coincidences, these two men with such complementary names and talents *did* meet on 4 May 1904 at the Midland Hotel, Manchester. Henry Royce, engineer and perfectionist, had just started producing probably the best car on the road at the time. Charles Rolls, aristocratic racing driver and car salesman, was on the lookout for a good British-made car to sell at his smart showrooms in Fulham, London. A man called Henry Edmunds knew them both and introduced them. Rolls was so impressed with Royce's car that he drove all the way from Manchester to London in order to drag his business partner out of bed to see it. And then ordered nineteen.

Those are the bones of the story. For the fascinating details read on.

The Hon. Charles Stewart Rolls 1877–1910

Charles Rolls was killed in an air crash less than six years after his first meeting with Royce in Manchester. But by that time he'd already done enough to make sure his name would never disappear from the badge on the radiator of the best car in the world.

By 1910 he, more than anyone else, had set up the sporty and aristocratic Rolls-Royce image. Being sporty and aristocratic himself, he was ideally suited to the task. Rolls was a widely renowned racing driver even before he met Royce, fanatically enthusiastic about all sorts of dangerous transport – fast cars, aircraft, balloons – and determined to make his mark in the car world. It was his ambition to have a motor car connected with his name 'so that in future it might be a household word just as much as Broadwood or Steinway in connection with pianos'.

He was the third son of Lord Llangattock, educated at Eton and Cambridge, where he studied mechanical engineering and became the first undergraduate to own a car – a Peugeot.

Soon he started racing cars and soon after that winning races. To get the money he needed to support his racing he set up in the car sales and repair business in Fulham. C. S. Rolls & Co. was very successful selling a variety of cars, almost all of them foreign and most of them made by Panhard. By 1903 Rolls was looking for somebody, preferably British, who could supply him with reliable cars to supersede the Panhards in his showroom. Thanks to Henry Edmunds, fellow member of the Royal Automobile Club and shareholder in Royce & Co. Ltd, he found the very man.

H. Royce, Mechanic
1863–1933

(*See page 180*)

There is an attractive but unproven story that the 14-year-old Henry Royce, then working as a messenger boy, delivered the telegram to John Allen Rolls's home in Mayfair, London, telling him of the birth of his third son Charles. Unproven, but quite possible, as the Rolls's home was on Henry's weary West End beat.

Royce was born in Alwalton, near Peterborough, Cambridgeshire, the son of an impoverished miller who died in the workhouse when Henry was only 9. The chance for an escape from penury and a succession of dead-end jobs (like delivering telegrams) came when a generous aunt offered to pay for his apprenticeship with the Great Northern Railway. Although he finished only three years of the five-year apprenticeship because his aunt's money ran out, he learned enough to start himself on a career as an engineer.

Working for one of the companies that pioneered electric lighting in England, and studying at night school, he learned more or less all there was to know about electrical engineering.

In 1884, with a capital of £70, Royce and his fellow electrical engineer, Ernest Claremont, set up their own company in Manchester. They started off producing arc lamps, lamp holders and, the thing that set them up once and for all, a bestselling electric doorbell. They went on to become prosperous on an output of dynamos, switchgear and electric cranes.

At the age of 40 Royce took the plunge and bought his first car. He was quite impressed, but characteristically decided he could do a better job himself. By the end of 1903 Royce had built a 2-cylinder engine and fitted it to a chassis of his own design, doing much of the work himself and often labouring on into the night with his long-suffering apprentices Haldenby and Platford. He then went on to build two more similar cars, deciding that it was about time Royce & Co. Ltd diversified.

Royce was producing a superior all-British car. Rolls, 200 miles away, was desperate to sell such a car. The link between them was Henry Edmunds, friend of Rolls, shareholder in Royce

Rolls in his first car, a Peugeot

Roll's birth certificate

& Co. Ltd. For several months Edmunds tried in vain to bring them together – Rolls was too busy to leave his showroom and Royce was too preoccupied with making his cars to worry about selling them. Eventually Edmunds got them together for lunch at the Midland Hotel, Manchester. (Incidentally Rolls and Edmunds travelled to this, one of the most historic meetings in the history of the automobile, by train.)

Rolls ordered nineteen Royce cars for C. S. Rolls and Co. to sell and spent most of his time for the next five years demonstrating the Rolls-Royce cars in trials of all kinds. In 1906 Rolls-Royce Limited was formed and the Silver Ghost chassis appeared at the London Motor Show. Its launch and early exploits – including a 14,000-mile non-stop test – made the reputation of Rolls-Royce in a matter of months.

Royce now concentrated on developing the car that was already burdened with the title 'the Best Car in the World'.

Rolls, having sorted out motoring, was looking for a new challenge.

'[Rolls] remarked, not long ago, that for him motoring was no longer pleasurable because being such a reliable mode of travel it had become positively monotonous. If it had not been for the excitements in connection with aerial navigation, he would, he declared, have longed for the old days when, undertaking a road journey, it was the regular experience to spend most of the time under the car.' (*Morning Post*, 13 July 1910)

*   *   *

Rolls was the first British aviator to fly more than half a mile. He was the first British aviator to cross the English Channel and the first of any nationality to cross and recross it. Then, on 12 July 1910, he became the first British aviator to die in a powered plane crash when his Wright biplane broke up in the air at a Bournemouth air display.

Royce lived on until 1933 to produce not only a series of very fine cars but also some very good stories.

. . . and Claude Johnson

In 1977 a play by William Douglas Home called *Rolls Hyphen Royce*, starring Wilfred Hyde-White, was put on in London's West End. It was about a man whose name comes up quite a few times in the stories that follow – Claude Johnson.

Johnson was a partner in Rolls's Fulham car business and in due course a partner in Rolls-Royce. Most of the great public relations ideas that shaped the Rolls-Royce image were his. It was Johnson's idea to plate the first 40/50 h.p. Rolls-Royce in silver and aluminium and christen it the Silver Ghost for its first

Rolls & Co.'s "Populaire" Car.

"A Marvellous Hill-Climber."

SPECIFICATION.

Motor.	6 h.p. de Dion or governed Aster, water-cooled by centrifugal pump. Throttle-control by hand lever.
Ignition.	Electric, with batteries and induction coil.
Gear.	Three speeds forward and reverse, all on one lever. Direct drive on top speed, with all intermediate gears at rest.
Wheels.	Artillery wheels, equal size.
Brakes.	Double-acting foot brake on gear shaft, and double acting internal-expanding brakes on rear wheels.
Steering.	By wheel, comfortably situated and non-reversible.
Tyres.	700 × 85 m/m licensed Clipper Michelins, Continentals or Dunlops.
Body.	Very comfortable phæton, graceful in design, and with abundant room for luggage.
Speed.	25 miles per hour.
Fittings.	Brass-plated petrol tank and lubricators. Three-way brass lubricator with pump. High-class brass trimming throughout.
Accessories (*all included*).	2 brass Paraffin Lamps. 1 Horn. 1 Tyre Repairing Outfit. 1 Tyre Pump. 1 complete Set of Tools. 1 Lifting Jack.

Price as above, 190 GUINEAS.

Extras.	Detachable Seat behind, £5 5s. If upholstered in real leather, £5.

C. S. ROLLS & Co.,
Automobile Engineers,
LILLIE BRIDGE, EARL'S COURT, S.W.

TELEPHONE: No. 1692 KENSINGTON.
TELEGRAMS: "SIDESLIP, LONDON."

What Rolls was selling before he met Royce

appearance at the 1906 London Motor Show. The 15,000-mile non-stop reliability trial was his idea as well.

*   *   *

After Royce's near fatal illness in 1911 Claude Johnson was the man mainly responsible for running the company. Royce never set foot inside the Derby factory after 1911 but thanks to Johnson lived on into the most creative years of his life.

F. E. Smith, reputedly the wittiest man in England (though not the most tactful) summed up Johnson's contribution at the unveiling of a statue of Royce in Derby: 'The real genius responsible for the wide fame of the Rolls-Royce car', he declared, 'is C. J.'

Below you'll find some of the most memorable facts and stories from the lives of these three remarkable men.

*   *   *

Henry Royce was fascinated by mechanical things from a very early age. At the age of 2 he was watching the spinning mill wheel at his father's mill above the fast-moving stream when he fell in. His father heard his screams and managed to pull him out just in time, thus saving one of the greatest mechanical engineers of all time for posterity.

*   *   *

One of Rolls's Eton school reports, which still survives, states, 'His thoughts are often far away in dreamland or vacancy, instead of being with his work.'

*   *   *

While he was at Cambridge, Rolls designed and built a bicycle for four – a 'quadruplet'.

*   *   *

Rolls was the first undergraduate at Cambridge to own a car: 'I often nearly got into a row for arriving back late at night after a breakdown; but I squared numerous venerable dons by taking them out in the car. A good many of these runs, however, ended up in pushing the car home with the assistance of my venerable passengers who often thus presented a very comic picture, arrayed as they frequently were, in caps and gowns.'

*   *   *

Royce's first job was as a delivery boy for W. H. Smith.

*   *   *

In 1899 Rolls was accused of 'driving furiously' in Kensington, London. He was trying out a car driven by an electric motor

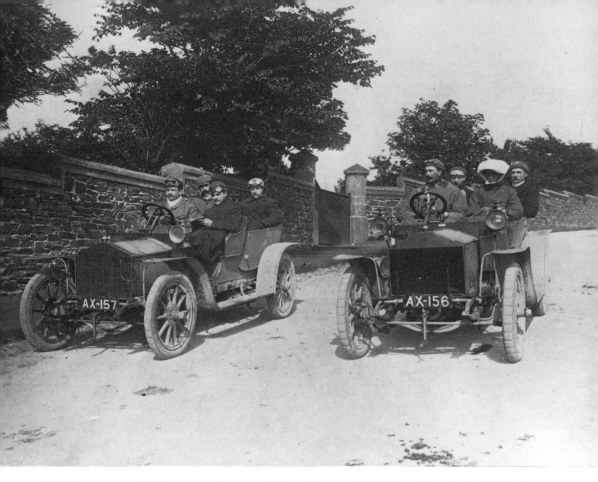

Rolls (passenger seat, left hand car) and some chums

and succeeded in getting an electrical engineer to testify that it was totally impossible for the machine to do more than 5 m.p.h.

*   *   *

Rolls probably did more than any other single person to popularize the motor car. In so doing he was up against such impressive figures as Queen Victoria, who hated cars because they frightened the horses, and the Marquess of Queensberry, who tried to get legal permission to shoot any motorist who endangered him or his family.

*   *   *

Royce used the drive of his home in West Wittering, Sussex, to test the first motor vehicle he ever had – a De Dion quadricycle. The rockery at the end of the drive was built to act as a fail-safe brake.

*   *   *

169

Royce and his partner, Claremont, both married in 1893. The two brides were sisters – the daughters of Mr Alfred Punt of London.

Royce's marriage to Minnie Punt was never very successful, and what with Royce's obsession for work and then his illness, they drifted apart. Royce's constant companion for the rest of his life was his nurse, Ethel Aubin. His last memo to the factory is written partly in her hand, Royce being too weak to finish it himself.

*   *   *

The electrical cranes made in the 1890s by Royce Ltd were copied years later by the Japanese.

*   *   *

Although he came from a wealthy family, Rolls never seems to have been keen to part with cash. He often slept under his car when on long trips away from home rather than pay for a night at a hotel. And once, when out with a girlfriend and her mother, he took them to a rather seedy café, saying, 'There is nowhere round here suitable for lunch.' 'Round here' was the West End of London.

*   *   *

There was a widespread story among those who knew Rolls that he often used to sneak his sandwiches into the Royal Automobile Club and eat them furtively in the lounge rather than pay for lunch.

*   *   *

Tommy Sopwith Senior once described Charles Rolls as 'the meanest man I know'.

*   *   *

Rolls was once demonstrating a Panhard to a prospective lady customer when a policeman on point duty in Tottenham Court Road, London suddenly shot out his hand to stop the traffic. On a wet asphalt road C.S.R. jammed on the brake. The car spun round, but he controlled the skid and, as they accelerated back up the road in the opposite direction, remarked, 'You see, madam, these cars are so handy you can turn them on a sixpence.'

*   *   *

A contemporary account of Rolls's demonstration of the Royce car to Johnson:

ROLLS: Get dressed, Claude! I want to take you for a run in a new car.

Sydney Ainsworth, destined to become Rolls-Royce's longest serving pneumatic tyre inflator, poses with the first Royce car

JOHNSON: A run in a new car? After midnight? Won't it wait until tomorrow?

ROLLS: No, it won't. I want you to see the car now. It's one of the best things that have ever happened to us. This car beats the Panhard hollow.

*   *   *

The first Rolls-Royce car was given its first road test on 1 April 1904. In the official report sent to the newspapers the date was changed to 31 March for fear that an April Fool's Day test might cause some adverse comment. The car did a 15-mile journey without any trouble at all.

*   *   *

The conservative and pessimistic Claremont, Royce's partner, always had a horse-drawn cab following him when he set out in a car for a business engagement.

*   *   *

Actually, it was 1 April
(see page 171)

One of the reasons why Royce concentrated so much on making his cars quiet was that he was sure that if motorized transport continued to be so noisy, people would always be prejudiced against it and the unrealistic speed limits would never be raised. A silent engine was more likely to result in getting the law changed.

*   *   *

Royce didn't have an office in the Cooke Street works, just a table and chair in the corner of the workshop. There he would sit working on engineering drawings, oblivious of all that was going on around him.

*   *   *

On the first lap of the first race in which a Rolls-Royce motor car had ever been entered – the Tourist Trophy Race on the Isle of Man, 1905 – Rolls wrecked the gearbox of the car by trying to put it into gear at speed. Rolls was unwilling to accept

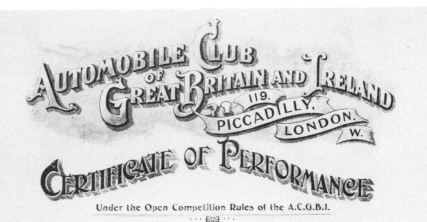

Automobile Club of Great Britain and Ireland

119. PICCADILLY, LONDON. W.

Certificate of Performance

Under the Open Competition Rules of the A.C.G.B.I.

THE INTERNATIONAL

TOURIST TROPHY RACE,

Held in the Isle of Man,—September 27th, 1906.

𝔗𝔥𝔦𝔰 𝔦𝔰 𝔱𝔬 𝔠𝔢𝔯𝔱𝔦𝔣𝔶 that the 20 h.p. Rolls-Royce

Car, entered by The Hon: C.S. Rolls

and driven by him

successfully completed the Course of 161 miles 240 yards, and was

placed First , twenty-nine Cars having started.

_____, Chairman of the Club.

{ Chairman of the
{ Competitions Committee.

_____ Secretary.

the blame and hinted at sabotage: 'I found a certain number
of broken loose nuts at the bottom of the gearbox, which, so
far as I can see, must have been put in through a hole at the
top. This is the sort of thing that frequently happens in France,
but I hardly thought it possible it could happen in this country.'

*   *   *

In 1906 Royce as Chief Engineer and Works Director, received
£1,250 per year and 4 per cent of the profits in excess of
£10,000. Rolls was known as 'Technical' Managing Director
and got £750 plus 4 per cent of the profits.

*   *   *

By contrast, Haldenby and Platford, Royce's original apprentices, often worked over 100 hours a week on the early cars for
£5 a week. Even then Royce would pay them grudgingly at the
end of each week claiming, only slightly tongue-in-cheek, that
they hadn't really earned it. On one occasion, when Platford
hadn't been home for two nights and had snatched a few hours'
sleep on a bench in his workshop, his mother turned up and
gave Mr Royce a dressing down about working her son too hard.

*   *   *

In 1906 Rolls won the Isle of Man Tourist Trophy at an average
of 39 m.p.h. He refused to take any credit for this victory, saying,
'As I had nothing to do but sit there and wait until the car got
to the finish, the credit is obviously due to Mr Royce, the designer
and builder.'

*   *   *

At the start of a record-breaking drive between London and
Monte-Carlo one of Rolls's companions found two half-bottles
of champagne and a large quantity of cold tea in the car. 'The
champagne is for me and the tea is for the rest of you,' explained
Charles without a flicker.

*   *   *

To what did Royce attribute the early racing success of Rolls-
Royce? 'To a combination of 2 per cent improvements in every
feature of the car over the best corresponding feature of any
other engaged, including the attainment of reliability.'

*   *   *

Claude Johnson had a genius for publicity. When the first 40/50
h.p. Rolls-Royce was to appear at the London Motor Show he
had silver plating applied to all the more solid outside fittings
of the car. Then he had the bodywork painted with aluminium
paint. The whole car looked very striking, and someone at the

works suggested that it should be called the 'Silver Ghost' – a name that was to continue in use for nearly twenty years and was to be echoed in later Rolls-Royce model names right up to today's Silver Spirit. This car – chassis number 60551 – is the only true Silver Ghost: other cars were known officially as 40/50s (a reference to their horsepower) and came to be called Silver Ghosts only to avoid confusion after the advent of the new Phantom.

*   *   *

Another of Johnson's great public relations ideas was a non-stop reliability trial of several thousand miles. The main scheme was to drive from London to Scotland, take part in the Scottish reliability trials and go on non-stop back to London. Then, still without stopping, the car would tour a number of provincial cities. The trial went smoothly for the first 600 miles, with a team of drivers (including Rolls and Johnson) at the wheel. Then the car halted for several minutes when a petrol tap vibrated shut. Once this was put right the car went on, day and night (except Sundays), for two months, covering a total of 15,000 miles, over 14,000 without a stop.

*   *   *

Rolls was given to doing impressions of music-hall favourites of the time. On one occasion, after taking a car for a drive to test a new braking system, he pulled the car to a dead stop in front of Royce and began a recitative in the voice and manner of Dan Leno, starting with the words 'Call that a brake?' Royce was not amused.

*   *   *

In 1911, at the age of 48, Royce was told that he had only three weeks to live. He died in 1933.

*   *   *

Johnson issued a challenge to all other motor manufacturers to pit their cars against the Silver Ghost in a gruelling 15,000-mile trial, including a 200-mile race round Brooklands, a race track in Surrey. He promised to put down £1,000 on the Rolls-Royce side if the challenger would do the same; the winner would take the cash. No one took up the challenge.

*   *   *

Rolls was the second Englishman to fly (the first was Griffith Brewster) and the first Englishman to own a private aircraft.

*   *   *

175

Rolls's last take-off

A few minutes later

Rolls's last journey

The car that towed Rolls's wrecked plane away after his fatal crash was, ironically, a Silver Ghost.

*   *   *

Royce worked unreasonably hard and conscientiously all his life and expected everyone who worked for Rolls-Royce to do the same. Company discipline controlled even the workers' visits to the lavatory: each man was given a token on arriving at work which entitled him to one 15-minute visit. A doctor's note was the only way to get any more.

*   *   *

Ruthless though he was in his treatment of people whose work didn't come up to standard, Royce was equally passionate about giving praise where it was due: a report he wrote on an electrical speed indicator ends, '... and we ought to thank the winder for having produced such neat winding on this model.'

*   *   *

He never expected any of his workmen to do anything he couldn't do himself: he once filed a perfectly hexagonal nut without the aid of measuring instruments. When it was measured, each of the six sides proved to be identical.

*   *   *

177

Royce thought that all leisure pursuits were a waste of time. He did, however, indulge in a sort of gardening, believing that growing vegetables was a productive (and therefore worthwhile) activity. Because the only time he had free was usually at night, he rigged up a generator and an array of lights so that he could garden in the dark.

*   *   *

At the Derby factory Royce noticed a group of workmen standing around idle. When he asked them why they were doing nothing, they said that the toilet was blocked and they were waiting for a plumber to clear it. Royce took his jacket off, rolled up his sleeves and disappeared into the toilet. He came out a few minutes later, having cleared the blockage with his bare hands.

*   *   *

Royce once noticed that a screw had come out of one of the hinges of his garden gate. He found a replacement, but as he examined it he realized how badly it was designed. He made a quick sketch of how he thought the screw should be made, deciding to get the factory to turn a few out by hand for him. Then he found that the blade of the screwdriver was worn and needed sharpening, so he returned to his workshop to attend to it. As he used his grindstone, he noticed that it squeaked as it turned. So he took out the bearings underneath the grindstone and oiled them. As he reached the door of the workshop, the screwdriver in one hand, the screw in the other, he found he'd taken so long getting things ready that it was now too dark to repair the gate.

*   *   *

Having found a minor imperfection in an engine block, Royce destroyed eleven more from the same batch with a hammer to ensure that they wouldn't be used.

*   *   *

Whenever Royce was looking for a new cook he would ask applicants to boil a few pounds of potatoes for him. If they boiled them all together, he turned them down. If they sorted them into small and large and boiled them separately – large potatoes taking longer than small to be perfectly cooked – he hired them.

*   *   *

Royce's inflexible maxim: 'There is no safe way of judging anything except by experiment.'

*   *   *

Royce used to test his cars the hard way – by towing concrete kerbstones behind them.

* * *

In a London restaurant a waiter approaching Royce with a creaking trolley found a new design for the wheels sketched on the back of the menu.

* * *

His greatest talent was improving and refining existing engineering ideas rather than inventing completely new ones. He once said, perhaps over-modestly, 'I invent nothing. Inventors go broke.'

* * *

Claremont had a notice put in front of the passenger seat of his Royce car: 'If the car breaks down, please do not ask a lot of silly questions.'

* * *

'You can't be an engineer', Royce once said, 'and go to church.'

* * *

At one time Royce was determined to replace the characteristic radiator of the Rolls-Royce with something more streamlined. Claude Johnson went to great lengths to change his mind. Eventually aesthetics prevailed over aerodynamics and the square radiator stayed.

* * *

Nothing escaped Royce's mania for simplicity and directness. On his orders, the words 'advance' and 'retard' on the ignition control lever were replaced by the more Anglo-Saxon 'early' and 'late'.

* * *

While trying out an experimental chassis near his home in the South of France, Royce used the horn and became angry when it stuck. He immediately issued instruction to the works that henceforth all horn buttons must have gold contacts. To this day Rolls-Royce horn-button contacts are made of a special alloy of gold and silver, even though it is now no longer strictly necessary.

* * *

Royce was always known simply as 'R' at the factory.

* * *

In 1930 Royce was made a baronet. He chose as his motto 'Fortis et prudens simul' (Bravery and prudence together) and elected

179

to be called 'Sir Frederick Henry Royce of Seaton in the County of Rutland', establishing a link with the place where his grandfather had been born and his father had once lived.

*   *   *

To the end of his days he always signed himself 'H. Royce, Mechanic', even after his baronetcy.

*   *   *

After a conversation in which Royce said that he was proud of every job he did, as long as it was done well, his friend, the artist Eric Gill, offered to carve a motto in the fireplace of Royce's West Wittering home: 'Quidvis recte factum: quamvis humile praeclarum.' It's odd that Royce let him carve it in Latin, a language he didn't understand when he would doubtless have preferred it in plain English: 'Whatever is rightly done, however humble, is noble.' The Latin phrase later became the motto of the company.

*   *   *

After singing the praises of Rolls-Royce cars over tea with Henry Royce, an aristocratic lady asked, as an afterthought, 'But Sir Henry, what would happen if the factory at Derby produced a bad car?' Sir Henry answered, 'Madam, the man on the gate would not let it out of the works.'

*   *   *

'I have only one regret,' said Royce as he lay dying, 'that I have not worked harder.'

*   *   *

In 1913 the Rolls-Royce board passed a resolution that declared they would never be involved in the making of aero-engines. Royce immediately went home and started to design one – the engine that became the highly successful Eagle.

*   *   *

The only occasion on which he used capital letters in his memos: 'MY GREAT MOTTO FOR GREAT BRITAIN AND OURSELVES IS MASS PRODUCTION AND QUALITY. UNLESS WE DO THIS WE ARE FATED. SO LET US DO IT BEFORE IT IS TOO LATE BECAUSE AT THE MOMENT ENGLAND CANNOT TRULY BOAST OF EITHER.'

*   *   *

A plaque on the wall of Royce's villa in Le Canadel bears this inscription: 'A la mémoire de Sir Henry Royce, mécanicien (1863–1933). Le Canadel et ses hivers cléments lui ont permis, entre 1911 et 1931, d'y concevoir et accomplir, pour

A la mémoire de
Sir Henry Royce
Mécanicien
(1863-1933)

Le Canadel et ses hivers cléments lui
ont permis entre 1911 et 1931, d'y concevoir
et accomplir, pour l'automobile comme pour
l'aviation, des moteurs et des machines
sous le signe de la perfection

The plaque on the wall on Royce's villa at Le Canadel

l'automobile, comme pour l'aviation, des moteurs et des machines sous le signe de la perfection.'

*   *   *

Although he designed some of the great aero-engines of all time Royce never travelled in an aircraft.

*   *   *

Royce left £112,000 in his will, mostly to his faithful nurse, Ethel Aubin.

*   *   *

Just inside the main entrance of the offices at the Rolls-Royce factory in Crewe, Cheshire, there is a bust of Henry Royce facing one of Charles Rolls. For many years the bust of Royce stood in No. 1 shop at the Derby factory and contained his ashes, until they were sent to Alwalton Church, where Royce had been christened.

*   *   *

It is often thought that the colour of the Rolls-Royce badge was changed from red to black after Henry Royce's death as a mark of respect. This is not so. It was in fact Royce's own decision to alter the colour, the last decision he ever made for the company. The change was made for aesthetic reasons: some customers complained that the red badge often clashed with the colour of the car. The Prince of Wales was particularly outspoken on the subject.

*   *   *

181

Royce and the woman who
helped him write his
last memo – Ethel Aubin

Royce's hand-written memos have been collected into nine leather-bound volumes kept under lock and key at Crewe – an inspiration to engineers for generations to come.

* * *

Henry Ford: 'Royce was the only man to put heart into an automobile.'

* * *

Royce spent his last day on earth making designs for a new shock absorber.

Index

"This Window commemorates the Pilots of the Royal Air Force who in the Battle of Britain turned the work of our hands into the salvation of our Country"

———

This Memorial Window was unveiled by Marshal of the R.A.F. Lord Tedder on January 11th 1949 and was designed by Hugh Easton. it is located in the Main Hall of the Derby Works of Rolls-Royce Limited

Order Form

If reading this book has raised your enthusiasm for the Rolls-Royce car to such a pitch that you too would like to become an Owner (if, indeed, you are not one already), you may care to take advantage of this form to place your order without delay.

Please deliver car(s) as detailed below.

		Number of cars to be delivered
Silver Spirit	£55,240	☐
Silver Spur	£62,778	☐
Corniche	£73,168	☐
Camargue	£83,122	☐
Silver Spur Extended		
Wheelbase	£140,000	☐
Bentley Mulsanne	£55,240	☐
Bentley Mulsanne Turbo	£61,743	☐

Extras to be included above standard specification. (Please contact Rolls-Royce for quotation.)

TOTAL

Please send cash with order or cheque payable to Rolls-Royce Motors Limited.

Full name . . . .

Address . . . .

Tel. no. . . . .

(Prices correct at time of publication. Rolls-Royce reserve the right to change price or specification without prior notice.)